OUT

OF

BODY

OUT

OF

BODY

NIA DAVENPORT

BALZER + BRAY
An Imprint of HarperCollins*Publishers*

Balzer + Bray is an imprint of HarperCollins Publishers.

Out of Body
www.epicreads.com

Library of Congress Control Number: 2023936926
ISBN 978-0-06-325571-5

Typography by Julia Tyler
23 24 25 26 27 LBC 5 4 3 2 1
First Edition

To all the Black girls who've ever felt like who you are isn't enough. It is, and you're amazing. Shine bright!

SHE CAN NO LONGER delay the thing she dreads.

She eases a navy blue duffel bag from under the motel bed, unzips it, and stares down at its contents. The metal case on top is a small, shiny black square—something that might normally contain her charcoal pencils and blending stumps. She wants to shove the bag back under the bed and flee the motel room. She should destroy the case. She should hurl it into a river or a fire or grab a fucking hammer and bash what's inside it to pieces. But she can't, because she needs it. She needs it even more than the stack of cash buried deeper in the bag.

It is time to act.

She will not let guilt eat at her. So, instead of destroying the case, she snaps it open and checks that everything she needs is inside. It is.

Her phone buzzes, vibrating loudly from its place on the dusty dresser. She abandons the duffel on the carpet, wipes her hands against her jeans—they always feel grimy after she touches the metal case—and grabs the phone. The dingy floral comforter reeks of cigarettes and must. She refuses to sleep beneath it.

What time are you coming over? the text reads. **So excited!**

Although she promised herself she will not feel guilty, her breath catches. The walls of the room seem to press inward.

The girl snatches up a second duffel bag from the bed. This one contains her sketchbook and enough clothes to last her a week. She hoists it across her back, then zips the other bag and hauls it onto her right shoulder.

On my way now, she types. **Can't wait!**

She grabs the motel key that hangs on the hook beside the door to turn it in when she checks out. After tonight, she won't be needing the room anymore.

One

"Getting jitters?" LC asks me.

I tear my gaze from the black metal case sitting between us on my bed. "No," I lie, forcing a smile. "Of course not."

"You better not be," she says playfully. Her light brown eyes, impeccably made up with killer mascara and festive gold eye shadow, gleam with excitement. When she grins, the whole room gets brighter. It's this crazy, infectious thing that usually makes me want to cannonball into whatever thrill she's proposing. But what we're about to do tonight is different. Bigger than our normal fun. It also means serious trouble if we get caught.

"Everything is sterile, right?" I ask, trying to quash my nerves.

She squeezes my hand. "I wouldn't let my girl go out like that. I got you."

Boss up, I tell myself. Tonight is a crucial friendship test. The ultimate trust fall, in honor of our three-month friendiversary. I can't fail.

She picks up the metal case and snaps it open, pulls out a small, sleek piercing gun.

I finger the earring that dangles from my right earlobe. My ears are the only things I've pierced. Until now.

"Wanna know a secret?" LC says as she tears open an alcohol-wipe packet. She slides the wet wipe over the plastic part of the gun and its metal stud holder. "I hate needles. All types. I dread shots at the doctor. When I got this done last year, I was scared as shit too."

"Really?" I say.

"Hell yeah." Only LC could say she was terrified of something and seem even cooler and more self-possessed after copping to it.

She unfolds her long legs and scoots closer to me on the bed. She bumps my shoulder with hers. "Our matching nape piercings will be fucking epic and bold. Just like we are."

I smile and swallow my nerves for good because she's right. It will look fierce. And that's the entire vibe I want. The next time LC says *we're* epic and bold, it really will apply to the pair of us. Not just her, with me hopelessly trying to keep up.

The decision made, a jolt of anticipation zips through me. I've never done anything this wild before. Dyeing my hair its current shade of violet is the closest I've gotten. But it's time for an evolution, and LC is the perfect wingwoman.

"Okay," I say, "so what's next?"

She reaches behind my head, lifts up my curly hair, and pinches my neck.

"Ow!" I yelp.

"That's how we prepared folks for the sting in the shop. It shouldn't feel much worse than that." She clips a slim silver barbell into the stud holder. Her aunt owns a tattoo and piercing studio in Fairburn Heights, south of here. LC worked in it while staying with her last summer, so she knows what she's doing.

Originally, when she brought up the idea to seal our friendship, I suggested she draw us matching bass-clef tattoos. She's an incredible artist (I'm low-key jealous), and I thought it'd be perfect, since we first clicked over our love of the indie rap playing in Hyped Up, our favorite coffee shop. But LC made me realize that was too basic—tons of kids get matching friend tats.

I eye the barbell, imagining how it will look on me. It'll be hidden. *Unless* I want someone to glimpse it, and then when I pull my hair up, it'll be sexy and unexpected. Daring. Like me. The *true* me. Not the annoyingly vanilla girl I was before meeting LC.

And, most important, it will match the one LC already has.

We've only been friends for a short time, but I feel like I've known her my entire life. We bonded so hard, so fast, I swear best-friends-at-first-sight is a thing. We're Betty and Veronica, without the frenemy wars.

"This is going to be a little cold," she says, lifting my hair again and rubbing the alcohol wipe on my skin.

Creeeeak! I bolt off the bed at the noise of the door opening. My younger sister, Sophie, barges into my room.

I glower at her. "I know I locked that door."

She waves a hairpin in the air with a sly smile. "You did."

"Get. Out," I growl, throwing a fuzzy star-shaped pillow at

her head. "Right now!"

Her eyes snag on the piercing gun LC holds and widen with interest. "Ohhhh!"

I lunge for her to physically shove her out, but the little troll dodges my grasp.

I'm so dead if she tells Mom and Dad. "Sophie—" I start.

"Y'all are getting piercings?" she squeals. "This is sooooo cool. Can I get pierced too?"

"*We* are not getting anything," I tell her.

She plants her hands on her hips. "Yes, *we* are if I'm keeping quiet."

"*Soph*," I snarl. "The answer is no. You're a little kid. So how about you keep this secret because you love me and you don't want to see me die, and I'll give you forty dollars, buy you that new video game you want, and do your chores for two weeks?"

She crosses her arms. "*Megan*. Make it sixty dollars, *Ghosts of Saturn*, a new pink Xbox controller, my chores for a month, *and* unrestricted access to your manga collection you *claim* you don't read anymore but won't let me touch. Then it's a deal."

"That's robbery!"

She smiles at me sweetly, her lone right dimple making her appear angelic. "If you cave about the piercing, it'll cost you zilch."

Zilch except my soul and my moral compass because I mutilated an eleven-year-old.

"Fine!" I grip Sophie's shoulders and march my pain-in-the-ass little sister out of the room. Between the cash, the video game, and the controller, I'm out a good two hundred dollars. I'll be broke until I get Christmas money next month.

"Sis is ruthless," LC says, like it's a good trait. "I'll pay half of what Baby Boss Bitch is extorting us for."

"You don't have to do that," I mutter. LC works an after-school job as a remote tutor for her spending money. I'm only giving up the rest of my birthday coins.

I sit back down next to her. "Okay," I say. "Ready."

Her hands brush the nape of my neck. I shiver as she gathers my shoulder-length curls into a high ponytail. She raises the piercing gun. "On three?"

I nod. "One . . . two . . . three!" I brace for the quick prick of pain. Nothing comes. "What are you waiting for?" I toss her a teasing, confident grin over my shoulder. "Are *you* scared now?"

She snorts, but I swear it sounds shaky. "Who, me? Never."

I'd gassed myself up before; the delay lets doubt creep back in. "You positive?" I say, suddenly hoping she'll give me an out.

"All good." LC grips my neck, and then—*bam!*—a million hot fire pokers stab into my skin. I clench my teeth so my parents don't hear me shriek.

"I thought you said it wouldn't hurt this bad," I gasp. I legit wanna cry.

LC leans forward and smooches my cheek. "You would've chickened out if I told you the truth." A second later, I hear the snap of a picture.

"You are so badass! Look!" she says, showing me her phone.

I gawk at the pic of my newly pierced neck. It's a whole vibe. Boring, plain Megan? She's ghost. Gone. The best-friend gods did their thing when they schemed for me and LC to collide at Hyped Up's pickup counter. Me thinking she swiped my secret-menu frap drink changed my life.

"Are you mad at me?" she asks.

I look at LC like she sprouted tentacles. "No! It's gorgeous! I love you. You're the freaking best for suggesting it." I throw my arms around her.

She stiffens in my hug.

"What's wrong?" I ask, pulling back.

Her features are pinched tight when I let her go.

"Nothing," she says. But she still has the same worried . . . or sad . . . or sorry look.

"You sure?" I say. "Because even if you think you messed it up somehow, which it doesn't look like you did, I can just take it out and we can do it over. No big deal." She's a perfectionist, so this is the only guess I have about what's upset her.

She shakes her head. "It's nothing. For real. I'm fucking up the mood. We still have more friendiversary shit to do tonight. You wanna call the rideshare so we can head to Nathan's?"

She finally smiles, but it stretches too wide, and her light brown eyes are flat. They're missing her spark—it's like staring into the empty eyes of a doll.

Two

As LC and I wait outside for the car, her funk seems to evaporate as fast as it arrived. She goofs around, practicing her twerk skills and knocking her hip into mine, trying to coax me to do the same. Despite my relief that her playful side is back, I snort and swat her away. Me and dancing (of any kind) don't go together. I'm like the one Black girl cursed with zero rhythm.

LC, true to form, doesn't give up so easily. She's switched from knocking our hips together to full-on shenanigans of an old-school butt bump. I relent a smidgen and meet her next bump midair. Giggling, I think about how we first met. After the frap mix-up, LC asked if I wanted to hang for a bit. I said yes, albeit hella awkwardly, and then we ended up spending the whole day lounging in a pair of beanbag chairs, vibing to the indie rap playing through the coffee shop's speakers, sharing our own favorite songs we pulled up on our phones, scoping the cute guys who passed by the shop's front window, and laughing at absurd TikToks and

YouTube videos. We had so much fun, it felt like the besties version of a meet-cute. I asked if she wanted to continue hanging at my house, and our extended chill session turned into a whole girls' night. She didn't leave my house until like two a.m. From there, we were a done deal.

I keep up the silly booty bumps until our car pulls up to the curb. Already in party mode, LC threads our hands together with a loud whoop and starts dragging me toward the Kia Soul before it even stops. The party is only a mile away, but it's too chilly to walk. A jacket would destroy the vibe of my off-the-shoulder plum sweater and ripped jeans.

"Megan?" the driver says as I duck into the cramped back seat.

"Yup, that's me," I confirm. LC settles in beside me while I tie my hair up into a high, stylishly messy knot, which I wouldn't have dared to do until I left my house. I peep the driver checking out LC in the rearview mirror. No wonder—she's hot as hell in the ripped black jeans and fitted gray sweater.

"So, yummy Nathan Ross?" she says, slinging her arm around my shoulder. "It's our mission tonight to hook you up with his fine ass."

I smirk, trying to downplay my major thirst. Nathan is beyond fine. We met him at the Music Midtown Festival in Piedmont Park last weekend, and me and him have been texting a little since then. He and LC have been texting too.

"You should go for him," I say. Tall, athletic guys with dark hair and brown eyes are her thing. They're my thing too, but friends don't swipe each other's prospects. It's an unbreachable tenet of Girl Code.

She shakes her head. "You met him first," she says, sticking to another tenet. "I'm stepping aside. Shoot your shot." She squeezes my shoulder. "Besides, I've had plenty of boyfriends before. You, however—"

I clamp my hand over her mouth. "We're not mentioning that."

She lets out a muffled laugh, then finishes her statement from behind my hand-muzzle. "You'veneverhad*one*boyfriend."

I flop back against the seat. "I need to change that."

She pats my hand supportively. "We *are* changing it. Tonight. My girl will get what my girl wants. I'll see to it." LC's promise almost makes me feel sorry for Nathan. When she sets her mind to something, she pursues it with a ruthless determination. Like the Music Midtown All-Access passes she won us for my birthday weekend. She dialed the radio station legit a hundred times for five days in a row during the contest so we could see Noize Crew, my favorite girl indie-rap group.

"That's getting annoying," LC snaps at our driver. I look and see he's staring at her in the rearview mirror again, real creep-like.

Caught, he turns back to the road. But as he drives the hilly curves, his eyes keep straying to the mirror. He's young, white, with blond hair and a frat-boy style (khaki shorts, polo shirt, and denim baseball cap turned backward). Between his clothes and the Georgia Tech Yellow Jacket bobblehead stuck to his dashboard, I'd bet money that he's a college student. Tech is a good fifty-minute drive south, but some students live around here in the Graysonville suburbs instead of in the dorms in downtown Atlanta.

"Are you famous?" he finally blurts.

LC frowns. "No."

"Are you sure? You look really familiar. I swear I've seen you on TV or something. Are you an actress? This will be my first time driving a celebrity around!"

I laugh. Of course LC has a swagger that makes her seem like a celebrity. I nudge her. "Pretend you are," I whisper.

She shifts in her seat, uncomfortable, instead of playing along. "You haven't seen me on TV," she responds tightly to the driver. "I'm not an actress."

The guy snaps his fingers. "You're a YouTuber. I . . . uh . . . can't remember what your channel is about. But I watch a lot of comedy skits, ghost investigations, and unsolved missing persons cases, so it's got to be one of those three. Which one?"

LC hastily unbuckles her seat belt as we pull up to Nathan's address, a two-story brick house on a hill, and thrusts open the door on her side.

"Wait! Can you at least take a selfie with me if you won't say?" the driver continues.

"Leave me alone, asshole," LC snaps.

She hops out of the car and slams the door.

I stare after her.

"Your friend's a jerk," the driver grumbles.

"She's not a YouTuber," I tell him genially. "She's . . . I don't know why she reacted that way. I'm sorry she yelled at you." I climb out of the car, hoping her blowup doesn't affect my passenger rating.

"That was kind of random," I say to her on the sidewalk. "Why'd you get so mad? Are you good?"

"I know where I've seen you!" the driver shouts out his window. "You were in the news."

LC ignores him and walks brusquely up to the house.

"You must have a doppelgänger," I joke to lighten the mood as I keep pace with her.

"Apparently." She continues to hold herself stiffly.

If the guy just had her mixed up with somebody else, she shouldn't be so heated. But this isn't the first time LC has behaved strangely. Like, she once told me that her arm was badly burned in a fire, but when I asked why she doesn't have a scar, she became all guarded and moody and snipped at me to stop with the interrogation. Maybe she was on the news due to the fire, which would have been traumatic, and that's why she got so upset with the driver. Instead of prying by asking if that's what's wrong and further irking her—or worse, triggering her—I drop the subject.

I loop my arm through hers and flash her the sort of confident grin she'd toss me. "The party isn't out here in the front yard. Let's get inside and find some drinks and cute boys."

"You mean cute boys like Nathan Ross?" she says, visibly relaxing.

We walk the rest of the way to the door arm in arm. When we reach it, LC doesn't bother to knock or ring the doorbell. She turns the knob and strolls right inside.

We're greeted by the sounds of thumping trap music and loud voices. The narrow entry hall opens up to a huge living room, where the furniture has been cleared away to create a dance floor. LC drops my arm and grabs my hand, squeezing us through the bodies crowding the room. None of the kids resemble the crowd I hang out with at school. The kids here are all more like LC. The kind you'd meet in front of an indie-rap or rock artist's festival set, like how we met Nathan. I don't know anyone here, besides LC and Nathan, but they *feel* like my people. Like a fun crew I could genuinely click with.

"Where are we headed?" I shout at LC as we pass the DJ booth, where a girl with rainbow braids and sparkly pink Converses mixes tracks.

LC pulls me to the kitchen, where Nathan and a cluster of kids drinking from red plastic cups hang around an island with an orange Gatorade cooler on top of it. "Y'all made it!" Nathan exclaims when he sees us. The berry-blue contents of his cup slosh over the rim. "Oops!" Twin dimples appear on his tan cheeks as he laughs and swipes long black curly hair out of his eyes. He takes a guzzle from the cup. "Grab some party punch to quench your thirst," he tells us, pointing at the cooler. The entire kitchen reeks of vodka.

I can't believe I'm at a party like this. I try not to gawk at my surroundings like a dork.

LC grabs two cups from the top of a stack next to the cooler and fills up one for me and one for herself. The alcohol stings my nose as soon as I raise the drink to my mouth. LC sips from hers while I toss mine back, shooting for the gutsier option and hoping Nathan takes notice.

LC clears her throat and nudges me closer to him.

"Hi," I say coolly. I can't be thirsty to his face. I grasp for something else to say so things don't get all silent and awkward. But, *gah*, it's so much easier to be funny and confident when we're texting than while we're face-to-face.

A kid walks up and slings his arm around Nathan's neck. "I'm Eric. Which one of you is Megan?" Eric is Asian, with short dark hair and a grin as cute as Nathan's.

LC folds her arms over her chest. "Why do you want to know?"

He squeezes Nathan's shoulder. "My boy here keeps talking about her. I had to meet the girl he's crushing on so hard."

Nathan turns bright red. "Ignore him."

Eric smooches his cheek. "It would've taken you forever to let her know, and I cannot take your angst much longer."

LC bursts out laughing. She jerks her chin at me. "That's Megan."

"So, are you into my boy?" Eric asks me.

I turn to LC with a *help me* expression—this is so far out of my sphere of experience. Thankfully, she swoops in, flashing Eric a mischievous smile. "I like you," she says to him. "You're my kind of person, and yes, she is into your friend."

Oh my God. My face burns with embarrassment.

Eric turns to Nathan smugly. "You're welcome."

Nathan growls and socks Eric in the arm. "Bro! Really!"

Eric rubs the spot. "Assaulting me is a weird thank-you."

"Excuse him, please," Nathan mutters. "He's an idiot."

"It's okay," I say, grinning so hard that I'm positive I look

15

goofy. I think of how LC would respond in this situation and put my hand on my hip, tilt my head, and try to give him a sexy look. I might look ridiculous, but I'm trying to be new, brazen Megan, so I fake it until my evolution is complete. "We both owe your friend. Glad we got the awkwardness out of the way."

"You two should dance," LC exclaims, then adds, "This is Megan's favorite song." A lie—it's just some random pop song that the DJ's playing.

"Wait!" I sputter, every shred of confidence evaporating. My fingers can finesse piano keys with no issues, but the rest of my body and a dance floor—heck no.

Dancing is one thing I *cannot* fake!

I tug away from Nathan. "This isn't my favorite song, actually. Maybe we can dance a little later when something else is on?"

He looks confused. "Oh. Okay."

"Megan is being shy," LC says. "She wants to dance." Then she whispers into my ear, "What the hell?"

"You know how I feel about dancing," I whisper back.

"You're tripping. It's not a big deal."

"For me it is," I hiss. A Black girl is expected to have mad dance skills. When she doesn't, it's mortifying. I made the mistake of attempting to dance one time at the Eighth Grade Carnival. I'll never make it again.

"Whispering to each other in front of people is rude," Nathan teases. "You gotta spill what you're talking about."

"We were talking about this wild thing that happened on the car ride over," I say. "Our driver wanted to take a pic with LC and swore she looks like someone famous or in the news. Does she resemble a celebrity to you?" Hopefully this will move the convo away from us dancing together.

He squints at LC. "Now that you mention it, she does look like somebody." He blinks twice. "I'm too drunk to figure out who right now."

"Don't bother," LC says. She puts down her drink so hard it sloshes and walks off.

I stare after her, taken aback.

"Your friend all right?" Nathan asks.

I shake my head, watching her disappear through a sliding glass door that leads out to the backyard. "I don't know. I should go check on her."

After working my way through the crowd lingering by the door and smoking outside, I find her standing beneath the edge of the deck, looking away from me. Her stare is fixed on a group of guys throwing a football back and forth. They've taken over the lower part of the sloped yard, lit by solar lights staked in the ground. "You okay?" I ask, risking a hand on her shoulder. "Sorry I brought up that whole thing."

She turns to face me, and, from her relieved smile, it seems her anger has vanished. She pulls me into a crushing hug. "I'm sorry for being shitty tonight. I'm just on edge."

"Want to talk about it?"

"Nah," she says. "Just stuff with my parents. What you *can* do is distract me. I know . . ." She pulls me farther under the deck, to a dark, empty spot beside a shed. My heart thumps at what the hell she's about to suggest we do. With LC, it could be anything.

She reaches into her pocket. "I scored party favors before I got to your house." She waves a small plastic baggie containing clear capsules filled with a white powder.

My eyes pop wide. "Are those drugs?" The naive question slips out before I can curb it.

"It's Molly. So not like a real drug or something that could hurt us. It'll only get us high and increase our good time." She pulls two capsules from the bag.

I take the one she holds out to me, eyeing it warily. "This is . . ." I'm about to say *extreme*, but then I'll sound like a loser, and tonight is partly about proving myself to LC. Drugs, though?

"You've never done Molly before." The way LC states it as if it's no surprise stings.

Not that she's wrong. I've never done any sort of drug other than weed, once, during freshman year. "Where did you get it?" I ask. "Do you trust it's not laced with anything?" I don't care how the questions make me sound. In health class, we learned that most of the Molly people score is laced with cocaine, meth, or bath salts. I am not messing around with any of those things.

"It's clean," LC says. "My supplier is a good friend. They wouldn't set me up like that."

She can't know that for sure. I stare at the pill, debating. My parents would go ballistic if they found out. And I have to wake up super early for a piano lesson. And I could possibly die from an overdose of a lethal additive. And I could go home and eat Sophie's face off. Okay, that last part's been debunked, but still.

You're reverting back to boring Megan, my inner voice pipes up. It's right. Megan who rocks the nape piercing is exactly the type of person who would pop a Molly during a party. She wouldn't overthink things. She'd just have fun.

I raise the capsule to my lips, and as I do, the thrill of rising to LC's challenge makes me feel like I'm already a little high. I place the capsule on my tongue and swallow it.

LC does the same with a hoot.

The plastic capsule gets lodged in the middle of my throat— the bitter contents make me gag. I take a swig of my party punch to wash it down. My heart races. But no other strange sensations happen yet. I look over at LC to see if she's feeling anything else.

She smiles at me with eyes that are almost teary, and says, "You're a great friend, Megan. Know that?" Her voice sounds reedy. "And when I can, I'm gonna make everything that's wrong about tonight right. Promise." Clearly, she feels the high already.

"You already have. We're good," I say, then close my eyes and tune in to my body, trying to feel what LC feels. A moment later, there it is—sheer bliss crashes into me. I throw my arms out wide and spin around in a circle, laughing. "This is amazing!" I squeal.

I spin and spin and spin.

My heart thuds faster in my chest. The world wobbles, and I wobble too. My stomach hurtles up my throat, like on the horrible Death Drop LC made me ride over and over at the county fair. Dizzy, I stop spinning, slapping my hands on my knees to catch my breath. My vision goes fuzzy and black dots whiz in front of my eyes.

The strong urge hits me to lie down and go to sleep. I collapse into a nearby lawn chair. I smack my forehead. I'm pitiful if I fall asleep at a party. Eyes half-shut, I slouch in the uncomfortable plastic chair for I don't know how long.

"Molly isn't supposed to do this," I slur. "It's an upper." Nobody responds. I twist around in the chair. LC is nowhere to be seen. Where did she go? When did she leave? I try to stand. The effort sends me buckling to the ground. My vision grows fuzzier. The racing black dots magnify in size. I can't keep my eyes open.

LC, I think weakly. *Help me.*

LC WATCHES MEGAN from behind the shed, pulse racing, anxious to get this over with. When Megan's body has been still for a couple of minutes, LC hurries to her and nudges her shoulder, making sure she's completely passed out. She is. LC scans the yard, confirms nobody is watching, then slides the wretched metal case out of her purse.

Opening it, she realizes her hands are shaking too badly to do the delicate maneuvers necessary. She pauses, looks out at the sky, and takes a deep breath to gather herself. Eyes on the stars, she wonders—as she often does—if a higher power is real. She used to think so, but everything that's happened and everything that still needs to happen makes her think there isn't a God. At least, not a benevolent one. He (or she, or they) wouldn't be this cruel to her or to Megan—a girl who might've been a true friend if things were different. If there was a God—somebody with the power to stop things—they would've been paying attention; they would've interceded a long time ago. LC wouldn't even be holding the metal case because God would've protected her before it got to this point.

Still, she says a prayer. A stupid little prayer. And then she begins.

Three

My eyelids are almost too heavy to lift, but I manage to pry them open.

All I see is more darkness.

I blink rapidly, trying to make it scatter. Blurry grayish-green replaces it. Skinny blades of grass come into focus, reddish clay dirt, and a line of ants streaming back and forth from a puddle of something wet and chunky and foul-smelling. I cringe, scooting away from what I'm sure is vomit. *Where am I?* My face blazes as snatches of the night's events bombard me. *Nathan's house. Right.* How long have I been passed out? It's still night, at least.

I haul myself to a sitting position and lean back on my elbows. The world lurches sideways. My upper body sags with a bizarre heaviness, as if bricks are resting on top of my chest. My right cheek and neck radiate fire. Ants must've feasted on me. *Great.*

I plant my hands in the soggy grass and push to my feet. As soon as I do, everything pitches sideways again. A massive headache erupts. The back of my head, the top of my head, behind my eyes . . . Everywhere throbs. I cradle my face, which feels over-inflated and tight, like a balloon about to pop. Tears rush hot to my eyes.

I'm alone in the backyard. Even LC is nowhere in sight.

Did she leave me?

I rub my head. It hurts so bad. Friends don't ditch each other at parties—that's basic Girl Code. LC wouldn't commit such a serious breach. I look around the dark, grassy slope again, making sure I'm not missing her. Nope. Maybe she's in the bathroom? Or went inside to get help?

There are a couple of outdoor safety lights on near the deck but no lights on in the house, meaning it's long past my midnight curfew. I stumble to the back door, barely able to stay upright. The door is locked. I bang on it, but nobody comes—not LC or anyone else. Where is she? It's so late, I likely have a crapton of missed calls from furious parents. When I blindly grasp for my purse, the canvas strap that should rest across my upper body is missing. *Shit*. Please don't tell me somebody stole it. My phone, wallet, keys, ID—everything is inside. It is super screwed-up to rob a girl passed out in the grass. *God*, what all happened between taking the Molly and now?

Queasiness sloshes around my stomach. I fold over and vomit. A cold sweat breaks out all over my body as shudders wrack me. I clutch my belly, scared the pills LC and I took were laced with something poisonous. Then a chilling thought strikes me: LC might be suffering the same bad reaction and that's why she's MIA.

Home. I need to get home. When I'm there I'll call her, make sure she's okay.

I have no choice but to walk. But it's not only my head that doesn't seem to fit me right. The same scary sensation plagues my limbs. My legs refuse to work correctly. I make my way across the grass to the sidewalk in front of the house, wobbling like a newborn colt. The ground seems much farther away than it should be. Like I'm freakishly tall. I rub my eyes. My lashes are stiff with mascara that I don't remember putting on.

Every dark block I walk is endless. My house sits in a cul-de-sac at the bottom of a hill. I never thought walking *down* a hill would be such a huge challenge. I repeatedly pitch forward, unable to find my center of gravity.

Miraculously, I make it to the porch and stumble my way up the steps. As soon as I get inside, I am calling LC and then collapsing into bed and sleeping for the rest of the weekend. Not that I'll have any choice to do anything else. My parents will for sure ground me until I graduate.

I try the door, praying that by some miracle, my parents forgot to lock it. No luck. My thumb mashes the doorbell, and I brace for Mom and Dad's wrath as the door swings open. Mom stands inside the foyer. Her eyes are puffy and red. Dad joins her a second later. He doesn't look any less haggard. They've definitely been up all night worried sick about me.

"I'm sorry," I blurt. My words sound slurred and my lips feel tripled in size.

Mom scowls. "What are you doing here so late?"

"I know. I'm sorry I missed curfew. I—"

She cuts me off. "What did you do to my daughter?" she asks, without the sort of anger I expected. And there's no worry mixed in. Just that corny *where did my real daughter go?* bit.

"You're right," I respond, too groggy to even deal. "I'm sorry for missing curfew and for making you guys worry and for losing my phone and for waking you up in the middle of the night and for—" I cannot dig that grave and admit to doing drugs. I'm buried in trouble as it is. "For losing my keys. I'm sorry for losing my keys too." I move to step around Mom and walk inside the house. I just want my room and my bed and my favorite fleece onesie.

Mom blocks my path.

Footsteps pad on the stairs behind my parents. *Oh no.* If Sophie is awake, she'll see me trashed. That is the opposite of setting a good example for my little sister. But . . . wait. I blink twice at the person who comes into view because it isn't Sophie.

A girl. Violet hair. Black new growth at the kinky roots. Dark eyes. Round face, high forehead. Fleece onesie.

Me. It's *me* standing there.

I rub my eyes, shake my head. *No.* I don't want to be high anymore. I want the Molly all the way out of my system. I want . . . I want my parents to stop looking at me like I'm some girl they don't know. I want them to let me in the house. I want to go upstairs to my room and my bed. I want not to be tripping out on drugs still and staring up at a hallucination of myself on the steps.

Mom turns toward the illusion. "Megan, get back upstairs! Your father and I will deal with LC."

26

LC? Where is LC? My head spins with confusion.

Then I catch a glimpse of my reflection in the glass of the open door, and the air is knocked from me. I rub a hand down my cheek, leaning forward. I touch shaky fingers to the reflection.

It isn't my own face that stares back at me.

It's LC's.

Light brown eyes, sharp cheekbones, slim nose, full lips. Dimple in her chin and light brown skin several shades lighter than mine. I drop my gaze to my hands. They . . . they aren't my hands. The nails are the same dark purple that LC and I painted our nails before the party, but these nails are long and neatly filed. My real nails are low and uneven from how often I bite them when I'm anxious or restless. The clothes I have on aren't my clothes either. Gray sweater, ripped black jeans . . . These are the things LC was wearing. My heart beats so fast, I struggle to catch my breath.

"I'm Megan," I tell my parents. *"Your daughter."*

They stare at me, clearly distressed. Mom's eyes crease at the corners like they do when something alarms her, and Dad scrubs a hand along his jaw. The girl on the stairs in my dorky Shoto Todoroki *My Hero* onesie stares at me too, with no emotion. If *I'm* on the porch, and that really *isn't* me in the house . . . who is it?

"I don't know what's going on," I say. "Everything is weird and warped. But I am your daughter. I am Megan!" I reach out for my mother's arm, but she pulls away.

"Please move back a step, LC," says Dad, who has been silent up to this point.

"I'm not LC!" I cry.

27

He steps in between me and Mom, like I might be a threat. "We can call your parents for you, but you cannot come inside while you wait for them to pick you up. You may wait on the porch. I can wait with you. You're having a bad drug experience. You aren't Megan. You're LC."

"No!" My shout is shrill and unhinged, even to my own ears. "I'm Megan. I am. I'm not LC. I'm me. I'm your daughter." I take my time saying the words. The voice, though—it doesn't sound like my own.

Dad's dismayed expression doesn't change. Neither does Mom's.

I swipe at the tears on my cheeks. "I promise I'm telling the truth. I was born on April eleventh at 3:38 p.m. I was born at home because of a blizzard that kept you from getting to the hospital. We've lived in this house my whole life. There are notches in the kitchen wall beside the fridge where Dad still measures me every year because when I was six I saw a dad do it with his daughter on some goofy TV show and thought it was cool. Mom, we got the dinosaur piano that's in the formal living room for me to practice on when I was nine. Dad and Uncle Tony put those scratches in the wood floor near the stairs while struggling to get it into the house."

"That's a nice recounting of things Megan has told you, LC." Dad's voice is terse and exasperated. "Excuse us for a moment." He closes the door most of the way and turns to Mom. They try to keep their voices hushed, but I hear everything Dad says. "That girl is on drugs. She gave our daughter drugs. We should've never let Megan hang out with her. I knew she'd be a bad influence. She's—"

"I am not LC!" I shove against the door. "Let me inside!" But Dad holds the door firmly in place.

"Lincoln?" Mom says shakily. "What do we do?"

"Leave this house," Dad tells me, as rattled as Mom. "Right now."

"No. No. No. *No.* You're my parents. You can't not recognize me. You can't not know me!" I push and push at the door that doesn't budge. I wail and start beating my fists against it. I don't care if I break the glass. My parents need to listen to me.

"We will call the cops," Dad threatens. "We don't want to, but you're giving us little choice. Please, just stop and leave." With that, he shuts the door completely.

The soft click when it locks rips me apart. I stand on the porch, staring at the closed door and my reflection—LC's reflection—confused and terrified and sobbing. I want to bang on the door and scream at my parents to let me inside. But Dad's threat to call the cops stops me. I can't believe he'd do that and risk somebody possibly getting hurt. Are my parents really that afraid? Of *me*?

I collapse onto the porch swing I begged Mom to buy in seventh grade so I could impress that year's group of friends—theater kids—by inviting them over to run lines together for the spring play. In eighth grade, me and Ava, my best friend up until last year, spent hours sitting here, giggling over episodes of *Sailor Moon, Kamisama Kiss,* and *Demon Slayer.* See, I can't be LC. I *am* Megan. I've got Megan's memories, and I know Megan's entire life

29

story. *None of what is happening can be real.*

For a long second, my gaze snags on my feet. They look huge. I wiggle my toes. They shouldn't bump against the tip of LC's combat boots. My feet are two sizes smaller than hers. And my legs . . . Look how far my legs are extended out from the swing. I'm so short that my feet should just barely brush the ground.

And what about that girl, the one standing inside my house? She looked just like me, and Mom and Dad *spoke* to her. They called her my name. I couldn't have hallucinated her, not if they saw her, too.

Who *was* that?

GUILT TURNS LC'S steps heavy as she walks upstairs.

I will not feel shitty. Not for surviving.

Still, her brain unhelpfully dumps the memory of the day she and Megan met.

Megan called it a best-friend meet-cute. LC wishes it had been.

But there was nothing cute or coincidental about it. LC already knew that the Strawberry Crumble Frap was Megan's usual drink. She knew from Megan's Insta, which LC had pored over after hanging around the high school and picking out Megan as a girl who might be perfect for her needs. LC's eyes had been drawn right to her, as if she was waiting for her. Someone on the fringes, a little insecure, looking around as if she wasn't quite in the right spot.

I'm so sorry, LC says silently as she enters Megan's cozy bedroom. *If there was another way, I'd take it. But there isn't.*

This is the only way.

She drops onto the comfy bed, hating that instead of making things better for Megan, the thing she's going to do now will make things much, much worse.

Four

Rain begins to fall in sporadic, heavy drops. *Fantastic*. Then the skies rip open and a brutal downpour pelts the house. *Even better*. Clearly, some cosmic power is cackling at my expense. What other explanation could there be for how so far outside of the realm of normal the night has spun? I'm kept dry by the porch roof, at least, but it doesn't shield me from the icy November wind that kicks up. My nose, fingers, and toes sting like they're about to break off. I wrap my arms around myself. LC's gray sweater isn't enough to keep me warm. I stare down at it, willing it to be the plum sweater I wore to the party. I squeeze my eyes shut, count to ten, and open them again. The sweater stays gray. Freezing, I hug myself tighter. My arms reach around my back way farther than they should.

I'm Megan. I'm Megan. I'm Megan.

Maybe I hallucinated the whole encounter with Mom and Dad and that girl on the stairs. Maybe I never knocked on my front door at all and I've been sitting here on the swing all this time.

I stand from the swing and bang on the front door. "It's me," I shout. "Can someone let me in?"

A minute later, a light clicks on in the window behind Mom's potted fern to my left. The drapes are open, so I can see into the living room. Sophie stands beside the couch, staring back at me. Her dark brown eyes—the eyes we both got from Mom—are wide and frightened.

I've never been so happy to see the little troll in my life.

"Sophie, open the door!" I yell through the window. "Please!"

She's looking at me, and she is afraid of me.

"Please," I say again, softer, moving closer to the glass.

Dad appears at her side. "Get off our property!" he shouts. He folds Sophie into a hug and leads her out of the living room, then turns off the light. LC's reflection stares back at me in the window.

I crumple to the wood floor. Press my hands against my head.

I don't know how long I stay there, curled up and trembling, wracking my brain for an explanation.

I need to deal with the facts: Somehow I'm inside LC's body, and someone is inside mine. As impossible as it is, it's true. And I suppose that what makes the most sense is that the person in my body is LC—that we've swapped bodies.

Is that what's going on? Is LC inside *my* body?

But . . . why would she have just stood there on the stairs? Why would she have let my parents lock me out of the house?

Feeling like I've tumbled into some alternate dimension, I

stand and descend the steps. Rain soaks me. I shiver as I walk down the brick path to the sidewalk.

I have nowhere else to go, but I don't want to stay and have my dad make good on his threat to call the police. I walk through my neighborhood with no destination, resolved not to cry again. If I start, I won't stop. *Everything will be better in the morning. It has to be.* The drugs will wear off. After I get some rest, I'll wake up and everything will be normal. Or I'll at least be able to talk to my parents, get them to believe that this has happened to me, no matter how crazy it sounds.

I find myself walking alongside Ava's front yard. We haven't talked since the beginning of sophomore year when I started hanging out with the popular crowd. If I rang her doorbell, she would be so justified to slam the door in my face. Not that she'd do that. She's too nice.

Although . . . ringing the bell wouldn't make sense anyway, not when Ava would see LC standing at the door.

Instead, I climb over the short chain-link fence that encircles the backyard and veer toward the old tin shed we turned into our Geek Girls Club when we were thirteen. Ava still loved hanging out in it when we grew apart last year, and I'm sure that hasn't changed. There'll be a pair of squishy beanbag chairs I can sleep on.

I slip through the door and feel for the battery pack nailed to the wall. Purple butterfly-shaped fairy lights wink on. I loved the lights when we hung them in ninth grade. Decorating the shed was our special project. Sophomore year, when I dyed my hair violet, deciding an edgier vibe fit me better, I hated the kiddie butterflies so much, I couldn't stand to look at them. I wanted to rip them down.

Tonight, everything about the shed is comforting in the way old, familiar things from when you were a little kid are. Like a shabby stuffed animal. Lying on one of the beanbags, I gaze up at the twinkling butterflies and think again about the "me" I saw on the stairs at home. What the heck is going on in LC's mind if we really have swapped bodies? Her expression was blank. Why didn't she say anything? Does she actually think she *is* me, because otherwise why was she even at my house, in my pajamas, in the first place?

I shake my head, trying to scatter the insane thoughts. *It's the drugs. It's the drugs.* They have me imagining things that aren't really happening. I tell myself that over and over again, even though I know this body I'm in is too real to be a hallucination. It's the only way I can calm down enough to get some sleep.

I wake up to frenzied barking.

The side of my face is stuck to the vinyl of the beanbag chair, and for a glorious split second I don't know where I am.

Then it all comes back. Along with a sinking ache in the pit of my stomach.

I chance a look at my hands, praying they have returned to dark brown with bitten nails. What I see makes me close my eyes again.

The shed door creaks open. I yelp and sit up as Freddy, Ava's monster chocolate Labrador, barrels inside. He leaps at me, barking madly, knocking me off the beanbag. His rough tongue leaves slobber on my nose. It's his favorite way to greet me.

"Eww! Freddy. Seriously?" I shove him away. "Bad doggy." I wag my finger at him like I used to when he wanted to assault me with kisses.

Freddy rocks back on his hind legs, whimpering at the reprimand. His floppy ears droop. He gazes at me with those massive, sweet brown eyes that always softened me even though I am not a dog person, because, admittedly, Freddy is adorable. "Sorry for fussing at you," I mutter.

His ears perk up as he thwacks his tail against the floor.

"Hey, boy," I say, realizing something. "Do you know who I am? You do, don't you?" I'm the only one Freddy has zero chill with. Ava always said that he knew she and I were best friends and he wanted to be best friends with me too. "I'm Megan, right, boy?" I hold out my hand, which he sniffs eagerly, and he keeps thwacking his tail.

How messed up is it that the one soul who recognizes me can't talk?

"What are you doing in my shed?"

I look up to see Ava standing in the doorway wearing plaid pajama pants and a Cardinals Marching Band hoodie. She has on the Sailor Moon rain boots we both bought during Anime Weekend Atlanta two years ago. She stares at me, bewildered.

"It's me—" *Megan*, I almost say, then remember. I need to be careful how I approach this.

Ava's forehead wrinkles. "I know who you are. You're LC. Megan's friend. Her parents called looking for you two last night. Why are you in my shed?"

"I'm . . . I'm . . ." I don't know what to say. I suck in a deep breath and prepare to explain. If anybody will listen to my story and believe it, it will be Ava. She's as huge of a sci-fi nerd as I am. (And she still proudly displays it to the world, unlike me.) "I know this is going to sound impossible," I say. "But I'm not LC. It's me, Megan. Something happened at this house party I went to with LC last night. I was stupid and took Molly and passed out in the grass. And I woke up trapped in LC's body."

Ava stiffens. Her gray eyes narrow in irritation.

"Wait!" I rush to say before she can tell me to get out. "I know it's crazy, but it's true, Aves. It really is me. I went home last night, and my parents saw me like this and didn't believe it was me. And while I was there, I saw me—well, I think LC, in my body. I think we've swapped bodies. I need your help," I tell Ava desperately. "I need you to believe me and help me convince my parents I'm telling the truth." As I'm talking, I can hear how confused and garbled it all sounds.

Ava looks at me like I've lost my mind. "Come here, Freddy," she says. Freddy swivels his head toward Ava, then gazes back at me. "Right now," Ava orders. Freddy whines but trots to her side. She curls a protective arm around him. "Please leave," she says to me.

I leap up and grab her wrist. "I'm telling the truth! I swear!"

"Are you high still?" Ava takes a step backward. She tugs Freddy along with her. "Or is this some type of joke? I thought Megan preferred to pretend I don't exist. Why are y'all bothering me?"

"You know that ridiculous filler episode of *Fairy Tale*?" I say, framing things in a context she'll understand. "Where literally everybody swaps bodies? Or that episode of *Teen Titans* where Raven and Starfire switch? It's like that. I don't know how it happened or why it happened, but I do know I am not LC. I am Megan. And I need your help."

"This isn't an anime episode or a manga volume," she says. "You and Megan suck for this joke. God, why is she being so mean? *I get it.* She thinks all the stuff we used to like is dorky now. She thinks I'm a loser for it. I got that message when she dropped me last year. Why does she need to make fun of me too? Tell her . . . tell her to go back to ignoring me and leave me alone."

When she turns to march away, I blurt out the first thing I think to say that might convince her. "We used to sew our cosplay costumes in the Geek Girls Club on your gram's sewing machine. The first costumes we sewed were back in eighth grade. You were Batgirl, and I was Ironheart, and we created our own made-up story of an epic crossover event while we stitched them." I keep talking, trying the same thing that didn't work with my parents, spewing any tiny detail I can think of to make her believe me.

As I talk, Ava's hands clench. She turns, her cheeks bright red. "Tell Megan she's a bitch. Tell her I said congratulations, *achievement unlocked. 'Moon Eternal, Make Up!'* She's reached her final form, and she's the worst kind of person. Tell Megan I hate her.

I'm taking Freddy back into the house. When I return, you better be gone."

"Don't go!" I beg. "Call LC. I'll give you her number. She can tell you things are weird on her end too, and since she's in my body, her voice will sound like mine. That should prove the switch." The logic sounds flimsy to my own ears, but it's all I can come up with, and I'm desperate. "Or . . . could I just use your phone and call her myself?"

"Get out of my backyard. Now."

"Ask me anything," I plead. "Literally anything that only Megan and you would know, about stuff we did together. I would've been mortified to admit any of the hard-core fandom stuff to LC. She wouldn't be able to answer."

Ava flinches at my words. I know they're hurtful, but I have to make her believe me.

Then she shakes her head. "You and Megan are both pathetic."

Freddy trots behind her. Halfway across the yard, he stops, turns back to me, and whimpers.

Ava chides him to keep up. He whimpers one last time and follows her command.

I trudge out to the street and stand on the sidewalk, sweating despite the chill. If Ava doesn't believe me, and if I can't go home, where *do* I go? Even if I wanted to, I couldn't go to LC's house like she went to mine—I've never even been there. She told me her parents were really intense and she tried to get as much space from them as possible.

In the early morning, our neighborhood is quiet. No cars on

the street. No kids playing in front of houses. No people out doing yardwork yet. Suddenly, the absurdity of everything induces hysterical giggles. My Georgia suburb looks like a dark planet from *A Wrinkle in Time*. I bury my face in my hands, flinching at the unfamiliar curve of my cheeks. At the sharpness of the bones. At the skin that's a fraction too smooth. At the nose, too thin and too small.

I sit on the curb. The same questions run over and over in my head until I can't stand it anymore. I clamp my hands over my mouth and let out the scream I've been holding in. I scream. And scream. And scream. And scream. Until there's nothing left.

I look up at the low *shush* of an engine. A police car pulls up in front of me. A different sort of terror cuts through my breakdown. One of the two officers steps out. She's a middle-aged white woman, and she wears a scowl that makes me automatically nervous. I stay as still as I can and make sure my hands are in clear view so she doesn't reach for her gun because of something she thinks I did or I'm about to do.

"I need you to come with me, Jade," she says.

Five

I'm too shook and confused to question anything before the white cop dumps me into the back of the patrol car.

Her partner, a Latina woman with black hair pulled back in a ponytail, twists around in her seat to face me. "You're not being arrested," she says in a kind voice. "I'm Officer Moreno. My partner is Officer Lindley. We only want to help you, Jade."

"Who is Jade?" I manage to say, while fighting off a fresh round of hyperventilation. "My name is Megan. Megan Allen."

"We know you're Jade McCall," Officer Lindley says. "No reason to play games."

"A lot of people have been concerned about your safety since you ran away, Jade," says Officer Moreno. "I'm sure these last three months have been hard for you. I'm glad we found you."

I gape at them both. "What are you talking about? Whoever Jade is, I'm not her. Please let me go."

"You have nothing to be afraid of. Officer Lindley and I are going to see that you get where you need to be safely."

"This is a mistake!" I say, growing frantic. "You have the wrong girl. My parents haven't been looking for me for months. They just saw me last night. I live at 2305 Lake Livingston Drive. I want to go home!" I swallow thickly because, *God*, that's the truth. I want to go home, and I want this nightmare to be over. Although . . . if the police do believe me and take me home, my parents will tell them I'm not their daughter. Fear sinks into my gut.

"You live in Fairburn Heights," Officer Lindley says firmly.

Fairburn Heights? That's two whole hours away. "I live here in Graysonville," I say. Even if I do look like LC, why would the cops think I'm a runaway from Fairburn Heights?

"Look at this, please," Officer Moreno says. She holds up an iPad and shows me the screen. "This is the picture the Fairburn Heights department sent us. We know it's you, Jade."

I gawk at the photo. The girl is wearing a tangerine sundress and flip-flops. She serves the camera puckered lips instead of a smile. Her reddish-brown hair has wavy curls that stretch down her back. I finger the straight, chin-length black hair on my head. The girl in the picture is LC. But LC would never rock a sundress in her life. Or that loud shade of orange. Or flip-flops. She hates showing her feet—I always tease her about it. She also keeps her hair short because she thinks it's obnoxious and hot when it's long.

But despite those differences, the girl is for sure LC.

Which means . . .

Her real name is Jade? She told me LC stands for

Leighton-Callista—a too-long, bougie-ass name that irks her soul. That must have been completely made-up.

And she ran away from home?

My mind grapples to reorient itself around this truth.

Was *anything* she told me true? The after-school job as a virtual tutor? The jerk ex who is the reason she isn't on socials? The irritating, intense parents she claims she's at my house all the time to get a break from? None of this makes sense. The only connection she ever told me about in Fairburn Heights is her aunt, the one with the tattoo shop. Do I even know LC at all? Is the girl I've spent the last three months hanging out with completely fake?

No. That can't be it. Even if LC lied about running away and her name, she has to still be *my LC*—at least on the most important level. I *do* know her. She's my best friend. Our bond is freaking *Vibranium* strong. You can't fake that.

Right?

The white cop puts the car in drive.

"Where are we going?" I ask on a shaky breath.

"To the hospital first," Officer Moreno responds.

"Why? I'm not hurt."

"Our priority is your health and safety, Jade. Before anything else, we're going to get you checked out. Make sure you're all right."

The patrol car pulls up to the ambulance entrance of Gramercy Hospital in Midtown Atlanta. Piedmont Park, where me and LC were just hanging two weeks ago for the music festival, is about seven blocks away. Atlanta School of the Arts, where LC supposedly goes, is right across the street. I stare at the glass building, wondering if she really spends the school day there.

Officer Moreno steps out of the front passenger seat and eases my door open while also blocking my way like I'm going to bolt. She curls a hand around my elbow and guides me out.

Officer Lindley stands like a tower of doom at her side. She takes hold of my other elbow. Her fingernails dig into my skin.

I hiss in a breath. "Ouch!"

"Ease up, will you?" Officer Moreno says.

Officer Lindley clears her throat but does as asked.

They march me through sliding glass doors. The harsh lights spark a throbbing behind my eyes. We wait near the entrance beside a wall covered with plaques praising the hospital's excellence. Mom swears by Gramercy. She's a nurse practitioner at its northeast campus, and she takes me and Sophie only to Gramercy doctors. I use the knowledge to keep a scrap of calm. At least they brought me to the best hospital and a familiar place.

A Black woman—another comforting sight—greets us. She's not wearing scrubs or a doctor's white coat but navy pants and a beige blouse.

"My name is Cherise Johnson. I'm a social worker," she says to me. "It's nice to meet you, Jade. I assure you that you are in good hands. Nobody is here to hurt you or force anything on you."

"You can let her go," she says to the officers. "I've got her from here. We don't want her to feel trapped or like a criminal."

Officer Lindley takes longer than Officer Moreno to release

her grip. They both move behind me. I glance back and see that they're standing side by side—forming a wall between me and the busy entrance. So much for me not feeling trapped.

"Don't focus on them. Focus on me," the social worker says. "They didn't harm you when they picked you up, did they?"

"Of course not," Officer Lindley snaps. "That was an unnecessary question."

"She's a young Black girl. It was quite necessary." Cherise says exactly what I'm thinking, then turns back to me. "And I'd believe you if you tell me differently."

"No. They didn't do anything bad," I say. "Officer Moreno was very nice." As for Officer Lindley . . . well . . . she could've been less of a bitch. "How long do you plan to keep me here?" I ask the social worker. "Why do I need to be examined?"

"Three months is a long time for a minor to be away from home," she answers. "I want to get you into a bed, have an emergency medicine doc assess you for any physical harm, and then you and I will talk from there. I'd like us to have a chat about why you left home, and I'm also here for you to tell me anything you feel comfortable confiding that may have happened before you left or after." She gives me a spiel about how anything I tell her will be confidential, unless she thinks I'm a danger to myself or others, or if she suspects abuse, since she's a "mandated reporter." "Does all that sound okay?" she asks.

"None of this is okay!" I cry. "This is so messed-up! *Everything* is so messed-up!" When I step away from Cherise, Officer Moreno and Officer Lindley move closer to me.

"Do this the easy way," Officer Lindley warns.

"That tone doesn't help in Jade's situation," Cherise says.

Knowing I have no real choice, I follow the social worker to a private room directly across from a nurse's station. I'm positive the location is on purpose. More eyes to watch me.

The room is spacious, cold, and has an open blue curtain between its main part and the narrow entry where we stand. The social worker has escorted me into a hospital room, not a prison cell. But it sure does feel like the latter.

"Am I staying here for long?" I ask Cherise, hugging myself. "I just want my parents."

She leads me to the bed. "It's good to hear that you miss them. After the doctor has examined you and we have a chance to talk, I can give them a call and hear their thoughts. If going home seems like the best next step, we'll arrange for them to pick you up as soon as possible."

Her words, which are meant to be comforting, leave me feeling like I'm suffocating. She isn't speaking about *my* parents. Lincoln and Malinda Allen won't be coming to get me.

I force even, steady breaths because I'm on the verge of a new round of hysteria. A breakdown in front of a social worker will make everything worse.

Being probed by the ER doctor is uncomfortable and beyond strange. It feels like I'm intruding on LC's privacy. Seeing parts of her I shouldn't see. I fix my eyes to a spot on the wall, trying not to glimpse the imperfections and the secrets she'd want to keep to herself. A birthmark here, a small scar there . . .

After the woman finishes the exam and leaves, Cherise sits

in a chair at my bedside. "Would you like to tell me why you ran away?" she gently asks.

It's already warped that I'm supposed to be LC. Or Jade. I can't start making up lies about her life. "Do I have to answer?"

Cherise leans against the back of the chair. "No. You don't. But it'll be harder for me to help you begin to sort out what caused it, and I'd like to assist where I can." Something catches my eye, and I notice there's a phone on the table next to her. A phone! If all these people would just leave me alone, I can call LC. Start figuring this out.

"I don't need any help," I tell her. "I'm fine. Everything is okay."

She nods. "If you change your mind, my job is to listen. That's it. I'm *your* advocate. And, as I said before, whatever you confide stays between us if you want it to. As long as you aren't in danger and others aren't in danger, I'll stick to that promise."

"I have nothing to tell you." *I have nothing to tell you because I'm not who you think I am.* I don't know why LC left home. I didn't even know her real name was Jade. I wish she had been honest with me. I wish she'd trusted me enough to tell me the truth. Did she think I'd judge her? Tell people her secrets? I'd never do either of those things. And more than anything, I wish she'd told me so I could've been there for her.

"Do you want to tell me where you've been staying?" Cherise asks.

The question makes me wince. I really, really hope LC hasn't been staying on the streets. "I can't answer that," I say. It's the truth. *I can't.*

Cherise rises from the chair. "Okay. If you aren't ready to talk yet, that's all right. There's no pressure. Get some rest. We can try again later."

I don't want to try again later. I want to get out of here!

"Wait!" I say. "Could you please call my parents now? It's a bit of a drive and I really want to see them." The hospital obviously won't release me on my own.

Cherise hesitates, then gives a small nod. "I want to talk more, but your physical health is excellent, and if you're sure you want—"

"I'm sure," I say.

She smiles, nods again, and exits the room. As soon as the door shuts behind her, I grab the phone and dial LC's number with a clammy hand, heart slamming in my chest, praying she'll pick up. Instead, a tone blasts in my ear. "The number you've dialed is no longer in service," says a recorded voice.

I punch in her number again, making sure I press the correct ten digits. I get the same message.

It's this moment when the implications of everything hit me. *Really* hit me. A sucker punch I never saw coming. Disconnected phone. Unreachable. Silent on the stairs . . . LC doesn't want to talk to me. Did she . . . did she swap us on *purpose*? I don't know what I was thinking before now. That it was some sort of freak event . . . But the idea that my friend—my best friend—did this on purpose? That she purposefully stole my body and life?

I call my own cell phone. LC herself might have swiped it at the party, but even if someone else took it, I know my iPad is on my desk. The phone rings and rings . . . and goes to voice-mail. My parents must have grounded "Megan" and confiscated my electronics. Still, I leave a message, just in case: "LC, it's me," I breathe into the phone, low and urgent. "What the hell is going on?! How did we swap?! Do you know? Why didn't you say anything back at my house? That was you, right? I had to spend the night in a shed and then the cops picked me up. They think I'm this random girl who's a runaway. I need to talk to you! I'm at Gramercy Hospital. The one in Midtown. Room twelve thirty-one. If you get this, call me back here. Please. As soon as you can."

Next I call the only other number I know by heart, aside from Ava's. Our house phone. Someone picks up on the second ring. *Thank God.*

"Hello?" The high-pitched voice is Sophie's.

"Soph?" I rasp. "It's me. Meggie. I need your help."

There's silence for a minute. All I hear is her breathing. Then Mom's concerned voice sounds in the background. "Sophie, who is it?"

"Why is your voice *funny?*" Sophie whispers. "And why are you calling the house phone from upstairs? Are you trying to get me to help you sneak out? I can't. I'll get in trouble too."

"I'm not there!" I yell without meaning to. I continue softer. "I'm not upstairs. I'm not in the house. The girl in my room isn't me. You have to believe me, Soph. That's LC in my body. I'm stuck in her body. We . . . I know this sounds outrageous, but I swear it's the truth. We swapped bodies last night some kind of way. I need to talk to LC. Can you go get her and tell her to pick up the phone?"

"I'm not supposed to talk to you," Sophie squeaks. "And you're not Meggie. Stop saying that!"

"Is that LC?" I hear Mom ask. "If it is, hang up immediately."

"Don't go yet!" I plead. "Just tell me this one thing first. Did she attend her piano lesson this morning?"

Sophie pauses. "No," she says.

"See! She doesn't know how to play. That's why she didn't go. So, what has she been doing?"

"Umm . . . homework," says Sophie. "She's working on her Octavia Butler essay. She—"

"Sophie," I hear Mom snap. "Give that to me."

The line goes dead. I call back again and again but get the busy signal every time. The phone is clearly off the hook. I hang up for good. Defeated.

I replay the jacked conversation in my head, a slow burn of anger rising as I do. I told LC about my English assignment earlier in the week. She's the one who suggested I write about Octavia Butler! She knew all of this stuff about her and had read some of her sci-fi novels. Was she thinking ahead, knowing that she was the one who'd have to write the whole-ass essay? Because clearly she's going along with this swap as if she's truly trying to *be* me.

But why? And how could she do something like this to me? How could anyone steal their best friend's life?

Not to mention, how did she even *do* it at all?

I have to get out of the hospital. I have to get out, find LC in person, get answers. Get my body back!

But what if the social worker was right to be hesitant about calling her parents? What if they're the reason she ran away to begin with? Will things just get worse if I leave here with them?

Suddenly, I think about how every year, Graysonville High's counselors hold an assembly in the theater. They talk to us about *"teen issues."* Everybody groans, but Mrs. Chen always starts the assembly with one statement that most of us take seriously because of the way she delivers it.

Look to all the students seated to the left of you in your row. Now look to the students seated to the right. There are fourteen seats in your row. That means, according to statistics, two of you in each row will run away at some point before you reach eighteen. The majority of minors who run away do so because of abuse at home. Graysonville is a family. We care. We will keep you safe and help you if you come to us.

Praying that no one is about to come into the room, I swing my feet over the edge of the bed and rush to the door. I ease it open. Peek out into the hallway. Exits? Are there any close? I spot an exit sign to my right, at the far end of the hall. If I can just slip past the nurses . . .

"Excuse me? Do you need assistance with something?" a guy calls from the nurse's station.

"Ummm . . . no," I stammer.

"Please return to your room, then," he says.

Clearly, they've been instructed to keep an eye on "the runaway."

I have no escape.

"WHAT YOU DID last night is unacceptable," Megan's dad stresses to the girl he thinks is his daughter.

LC doesn't need to fake looking miserable.

"We're disappointed," Megan's mom says. She's seated beside her husband at the kitchen table. "Last night could've ended worse than it did. Someone could have hurt you, or the police could have busted up the party and rounded you up with drugs and alcohol in your system. You're too bright for that, and you have too much going for you. You have college and a whole life ahead of you to think about. Bad decisions can seriously affect your future. Do you understand the recklessness of your choices last night?"

LC flinches. Bad decisions have already seriously affected her future. Now she's paid it forward and jeopardized Megan's future too. She can't meet the Allens' gazes. She fixes her stare on a water stain in the wood table, wondering if the police have found Megan yet. And if they did find her, what they've done with her. It was LC who let them know the missing Fairburn girl was in Graysonville. She had to.

But, like she promised Megan last night, she's going to make everything right as soon as she can.

You are? a voice says. *How?*

Megan's dad gets up from the table and walks to the stove. A minute later, he sets a plate of the wheat toast, scrambled eggs, and bacon in front of LC. "You need to eat," he says, sounding concerned.

She isn't hungry. She couldn't eat right now even if she wanted to. And if he knew she hijacked their real daughter's body and invaded their home, he wouldn't be so nice. He'd think she was a monster.

You are a monster, the voice says.

LC bites the inside of her cheek. No! She isn't the real monster in this story.

To calm herself, she picks up the pencil lying on the table beside a sudoku book. She doodles on the paper napkin beside her plate, blocking everything out.

"What are you doing?" Sophie asks, poking the drawing.

LC's hand stills. She presses the pencil's point into the napkin so hard, the lead snaps. *Shit.* She's messing up. Doodling is not a Megan thing. It's an LC thing. She has to do better. She can't afford to be sloppy. Sophie is dangerously smart and has been hovering all day.

"That's a really good drawing of yourself," Sophie says. "When did you learn to draw that good?"

"LC taught me." The explanation comes easy because it's a lie that isn't a lie. "She's great at it, and I've been practicing."

Sophie grabs the portrait. She holds it an inch away from her face. She scrutinizes it, then does the same to LC. "You've only known her for three months. You can't get this good in so little time."

LC plucks it out of her hand and crumples it into a ball. "It isn't that good. And I watched some YouTube videos too."

"The piano is what you really should be practicing," Megan's mom asserts. "You missed your lesson this morning."

Panic crashes into LC. Megan being so good at the piano, good enough to have an upcoming recital as a part of the Atlanta Symphony Young Teen Musicians Showcase, is one thing she is still trying to figure out how to skirt around. She can't just declare that she is quitting. Megan has the type of parents who won't accept it. She will have to figure out something.

Despite the stress, LC hopes she can stay with the Allens for a little while. She's tired. So tired. It's also nice to have parents who care. To be a part of a real family.

Not to mention, making things right in the end is going to become more complicated if she has to run again.

If she has to run again? Who is she kidding? When she runs again . . .

If there's one thing she's learned, it's that you can hide from monsters for only so long.

Six

"Jade. I was so worried you might be dead!" A tall Black woman rushes to my bedside. I stiffen as she swallows me up in a perfume-laced hug. When she finally pulls back, she tucks the thin hospital blanket tighter around me and wipes her eyes. They're the same chestnut brown as LC's. Her skin is light brown—maybe a shade or two darker than her daughter's—and she wears jeans and a Spelman alumna sweatshirt. I give her a small smile, not sure what else to do.

A white man with blond hair and gray eyes comes to stand beside her. He wears track pants and a golf polo. It's an outfit Dad would wear on a Saturday. But he isn't *my* dad. I don't know what he or his wife might do to their daughter for running away. Cherise told me that she spoke to them at length and that she was comfortable with having them come here, but maybe they're just good actors? LC did say she has demanding parents.

Despite LC's mom's gentleness, I gaze at her and her husband warily.

LC's dad hugs me tight. "You aren't in trouble, and we're not mad," he says, as if he read my mind. "The only important thing is that we found you safe. Thank God somebody called the police."

I wonder who . . . *The rideshare driver.* He swore LC was in the news. That's why she got so weirdly upset. Maybe he figured it out.

LC's mom smooths my hair. I flinch at her touch. Hurt clouds her eyes. "Was it us? Did we do something?"

Did they?

She and LC's dad both look completely devastated. They peer down at me, waiting for me to respond. But I can't.

LC's dad pats my hand. "It's okay," he says. "Talking about things can wait until you feel better."

They both hug me again. LC's mom kisses my forehead. She hasn't stopped crying.

Cherise steps into the room. "It's nice to meet you in person, Mrs. and Mr. McCall. I'm the social worker you spoke to over the phone." She shakes LC's—or, I guess, *Jade's*—parents' hands. "How are you feeling, Jade?" she asks me. Each time somebody calls me that name, it takes everything in me not to flinch or shout, *My name is Megan!*

I paste on a smile. "Much better now that my parents are here. When can I go home?" As I say it, I feel myself breaking out in a cold sweat. Even though I know my only option for getting out of here is to keep pretending to be Jade, it feels like agreeing to leap out of a plane. Without a parachute.

"We need to first make sure you're one hundred percent ready for that, emotionally," says Cherise. "I'd like us all to consider you speaking with me more extensively as the next step."

Mrs. McCall cups my cheek. "There's no rush to go home. Dad and I will stay close by while you're here for a bit, if that's what you need."

I waver, wondering if it is safer to give them a reason to keep me here rather than risk whatever might be waiting for me at the McCalls. But then I have another thought: *This isn't an anime episode or a manga volume*, Ava said. But those stories are the only reference I have for something as absurd as a body swap, and in those stories, the characters are always running against a clock to reverse things. If too much time passes, the swap becomes permanent. I don't know if that same time principle applies to whatever has happened to me, but if there's even the slightest chance, I need to do whatever I can to fight against it.

"I'm ready to go home," I insist. "I swear I'm fine. Just take me home. Please." I clutch Mrs. McCall's hand.

Cherise studies me. There's a clock on the wall beside the TV, ticking loudly. Was it always so loud? I didn't even notice it before. I feel like I'm losing my mind.

"Could you please give us a minute alone?" she asks the McCalls.

As soon as they step outside, she says, "You haven't yet told me why you left home in the first place, Jade. That was a serious decision. You had a reason. While I don't want to pressure you to divulge what that was until you're comfortable, it is important for us to acknowledge that if you don't work through the reason, it'll continue to exist. Without the tools to cope with it or alleviate it, you may feel like you have to repeat your actions. If you suffered a trauma, or something, keeping it buried won't make it disappear. Does that make sense?"

I nod to try to appear as earnest as possible. Hopefully, Cherise was thorough in her job and triple-checked LC's parents, because I tell her, "It makes perfect sense, but I just want to go home. I can't stay here. It'll make things worse." I don't have to fake the desperation in my voice. It comes out wobbly and small and fragile. I *cannot* stay here. What if she decides I'm really messed-up and I end up in a psych institution for several days or weeks? I can't, not while LC is out there living my life. And not when this swap might have a ticking clock on the ability to reverse it!

"Can I go home now and do therapy there?" I ask her.

"You could," says Cherise. "If that's what you want and your parents agree."

"Yes," I say. "That's what I want. A therapist in Fairburn."

"We love you and missed you, Jade Bear," Mr. McCall says, making me cringe as he and his wife lead me out of the hospital's main entrance.

Mr. McCall hands the valet guy a red ticket, and it becomes harder to breathe because the next scary step is to leave the neighborhood, to leave *Atlanta*, with these people for a place that's several towns away. A couple of minutes later, the guy parks a white Range Rover in front of the valet stand. Jade's dad tips him nicely, then helps me into the back seat. Afterward, he helps his wife into the front passenger seat. He's the definition of polite

Southern manners. I wish that made me feel better.

As we begin the drive, Jade's parents are quiet. I get the sense they're trying to give me space. Mom and Dad would already be tag-teaming me with a bajillion questions and demanding answers. I don't see the intense parents LC told me she had. They obviously love LC—or Jade—a lot. Maybe they are decent people and merely have a twisted daughter who ended up that way all on her own. My anger toward LC spikes. I blink away hot tears.

"Is Megan a friend?" Mrs. McCall asks.

I jump. Hearing her say my name is like being shaken.

"Or is it just the name you've been using?" she continues gently. "The police told us you said your name was Megan when they found you after the anonymous tip. They said you gave them an address in Graysonville along with the fake name. Is that where you've been staying?"

I answer, "Megan isn't real. I made up the name and the address because I was scared."

My stomach drops. With the lie, it's like I'm erasing myself. Accepting the fact that I am Jade McCall.

Maybe you are. Body swapping isn't real. Maybe you are, and always have been, Jade.

Am I suffering some sort of break with reality, the result of some sort of trauma, like Cherise was worried about?

Which is more common, a psychotic break or body swapping? I think with cold dread.

We drive past the exit sign for Centennial Olympic Park. The giant gold torch you can see from the highway sparks a wave of memories. Riding the train downtown with Mom, Dad, and Sophie. Going to World of Coca-Cola because we all get a kick out of tasting the different soda formulas. Sophie and I playing at Centennial Park's splash pad in the summer and settling for the playground in fall or winter. Remembering these outings somewhat eases my panic, because these *can't* be Jade's memories. How could I be her and still feel this way—and know so much—about *Megan's* family?

More memories of outings at Centennial Park whirl through my mind, including the earliest that I can vividly recall, when I was six and had an *Alice in Wonderland* birthday party there. Nearly all of my guests came in costumes at my insistence. I loved being Alice so much that I wore my blue party dress for two whole days afterward. Mom dressed up as the Queen of Hearts. My best friend Sasha was the Dormouse. On and on, memories from the park play in hyper-speed as if I'm reliving them all at once in a few compressed seconds.

I am Megan Allen.

I *am* Megan Allen.

I feel the absolute truth of it, the absolute certainty that Mr. and Mrs. McCall and the social worker and the cops are wrong. Jade wouldn't recall any of these experiences. Especially not the ones with Sasha, who LC doesn't know existed. Abruptly losing my first and closest best friend ever is a wound that I don't talk about.

I *need* to talk to LC. A frenzied desperation envelops me. She's the one who gave me the Molly. She abandoned me at the party.

And she looked me right in the eye at my house as I screamed that I was really Megan. I don't care why she wants this; we've got to swap back. Even if I have to force her.

I lean my head against the seat and close my eyes, figuring out how I can get to LC in person, especially now that I'm being hauled about a hundred miles away.

But I don't come up with one feasible solution. Eventually, I just become drained and fall asleep without meaning to.

"Jade, honey?" Mrs. McCall says, startling me out of the shallow, fitful sleep. "We're here."

I open my eyes as the SUV pulls into a sweeping cobblestone driveway in front of a massive house whose facade is all glittering panes of glass. It's not Tony-Stark's-mansion huge, but it's definitely nothing I've ever seen around Graysonville.

Mrs. McCall opens my door and eases me out of the car.

I stare up at their beautiful, enormous home that could fit three of my houses inside its walls. *Oh my freaking God.* LC is rich. Like *rich*, rich.

Mr. McCall holds my hand. "Welcome home, Jade Bear. We're going to work very hard to make sure you never want to run again."

Seven

Mr. McCall opens a door that's one humongous pane of glass. Once we're all inside, he presses his thumb to the keypad above the slim silver door handle. After three rapid beeps, a female voice informs us, "Alarm activated in In-Residence Mode. Please disable before opening doors or windows."

The breath whooshes out of me at the announcement. I sweep a look around the white marble foyer; the mansion is no longer stunning or impressive. All the glass . . . The clear view *outside* it provides . . . The robotic voice telling me I've been locked *inside* . . . The home turns sinister. I shiver and fight the urge to hurl the heavy-looking bronze vase on the entry table through the door. "Jade? Jade Bear, are you all right?"

Mrs. McCall lays a hand against my shoulder, and I jump.

Mr. McCall gives me a smile that attempts to be comforting and kind. But there's a brittleness to it as he glances back at the door like he's afraid I'll bolt.

"Do we really need an alarm on?" I say tightly. I won't be able to so much as crack a window without the McCalls being alerted.

Mr. McCall's brows draw together. "You know we always use it, Jade Bear."

"I know, I just . . ." I laugh, positive I look exactly as unhinged as they think I am. "Never mind."

Get it together, I tell myself. But I have no clue how to *be* who the McCalls expect. Standing inside the ritzy mansion, I'm struck with how impossibly hard living this lie is gonna be.

I paste on a sunny smile and squeeze Jade's dad's hand, because one thing I can do for now is prove that I'm trustworthy. "I'm sorry I freaked a little," I say to Mr. and Mrs. McCall. "It's just . . . overwhelming to be back home after so long. I—I'll do better. And I love you guys. I'm so glad to be back." The words are so stiff, I'm not sure they buy them.

Thankfully, neither of the McCalls seem to notice. Mrs. McCall only pulls me into a hug. "Let's get you upstairs and comfortable," she says. "Are you hungry? I asked Phyllis to make one of your favorites for dinner: steak medallions!"

I wrinkle my nose before I can control my reaction. Another slipup. But LC claimed she was a vegan, like me. It's one of the things we bonded over—apparently one of her many lies.

"Is something vegan an option?" I ask, testing the McCalls a bit, trying to figure out what kind of parents they really are.

For a split second, the McCalls look dismayed, but after a moment, Mrs. McCall gives me an accommodating smile. "Phyllis can whip up a lasagna without meat or dairy products. How does that sound?"

"Delicious," I say honestly.

Mrs. McCall hooks her arm through mine. "Come on, I'll help you settle into your room in the meantime. I'm guessing you may want a minute alone and a little privacy after everything."

"I'd like that a lot," I say. I can't quite manage to tack on *Mom* at the end.

As Mrs. McCall walks me up a curved, gleaming black stair-case, I glance down at the huge foyer, and I'm stricken with a new worry. How the heck am I supposed to fake knowing my way around the freaking mansion? Jade's parents are handling their daughter with extreme care now, but they certainly won't continue to guide me everywhere I go. At some point, I'm going to need to explore on my own so I don't act like a guest in my supposed home.

In the second-floor hallway, there are framed photos hanging along the eggshell-white wall. Jade is in every one of them. Some-times she's by herself, but more often she's with her parents. Seems like she has no siblings, which is a good thing—fewer people to deal with. The pictures are from all over the world. Jade and the McCalls make silly air-kisses in front of the Eiffel Tower in one. In another, they're sitting on a glittering white-sand beach—in the top left corner, *Labadi Beach, Accra, Ghana* is scrawled in blue cursive letters. I halt in front of a third shot, the photo the cops showed me, where Jade stands alone, wearing a tangerine sundress and gold flip-flops. It makes me itch to ask so many things, to start to untangle which of LC's likes and dislikes were made up so she could get close to me and which were genuine changes after she ran away. Like, why did she change her hair? When did she stop wearing bright colors and sundresses? Did she shift from the bubbly, glitzy Jade in the photo to the much more low-key, hard-edged LC to appear cooler to me? LC's grunge-chic vibe *was* one of the things that drew me to her. It captured the exact energy I was always trying to exude. Was that earnest or phony?

"We had so much fun on that trip, didn't we?" Mrs. McCall says.

"Mm-hmm," I say, wondering if they really did. It looks like it in the picture. But even though LC was fun and adventurous, she also always had an undercurrent of someone dealing with a lot of heavy crap in her personal and family life. Stuff she refused to talk about. So what the hell happened between when these photos were taken and when I met her?

Did you really know your daughter? I want so badly to ask Mrs. McCall.

After Mrs. McCall leaves me in Jade's room to shower and nap until dinnertime, I close the door and lean against it for a moment, unbelievably relieved to be alone. Relieved not to have to pretend to be anyone but Megan for now. I give myself one minute to revel in the feeling. Then I get to work.

First, I scan the room for a phone or computer and don't see either sitting out in any of the obvious places—desk, nightstand, bed. They might be stored in a drawer, I guess, but more likely the

McCalls or the police confiscated them when Jade ran away.

Next, I dive into a search of the room, top to bottom, looking for anything that will tell me who LC was when she was sunny Jade McCall. And who knows, maybe there will be something that'll give me clues to *how* this inconceivable swap occurred. Maybe I'll even find evidence of what the hell drove her to do such an awful thing. A diary explaining it is probably too much to hope for, but maybe?

I start with the pristine white dresser beside the bed. A peach-scented candle and a framed print of an owl sit atop it—nothing else. The drawers hold only clothing—mostly soft leggings and brightly colored T-shirts, bras, and underwear. After rummaging through to make sure there's nothing hidden, I abandon it and move to the closet, where I typically stash stuff I want to keep secret. It's humongous—my whole room could fit inside it. But there are no keepsake boxes or storage tubs or even shoeboxes like I have in my closet. It's another impeccably neat room, with a mixture of vintage-looking and designer clothing arranged perfectly on hangers and grouped by color. There's a floor-to-ceiling shoe rack on one wall, filled with fancy high heels, sparkly sandals, neon flips-flops, and a handful of sneakers. That's it.

I go back into the bedroom. Riffle through the antique-looking armoire that contains a million earrings, bangles, and necklaces; a vanity with pastel eye shadows and lippies; and a night table with a stack of fashion magazines. I slam the night table's drawer closed, frustrated.

I head for the desk, the last place I haven't searched. I yank open its side drawer. There are cheer ribbons, an old academic planner, a report card with straight As and *no* art classes, several swim-team medals, and a scrapbook whose cover has an elaborate navy-and-cream crest with the words *Woodard College Preparatory Academy for Girls* printed on it. There's also a sticky-back Polaroid photo beneath the crest. In it, Jade is smiling wide next to a cute brown-eyed Black boy with dark hair cut short in a fade. The photo looks fairly recent.

I snatch up the scrapbook and flip it open on the desk. See more pictures—mostly selfies—of Jade and the boy on each of the first pages. I don't find names scrawled beneath any of the photos. But she's obviously known him for a long time because the photos show the guy and Jade ranging in age from teen years back to kids of maybe seven or eight. Which means this is someone she was *extremely* close with. Like *close*, close. Is he a best friend, maybe? A boyfriend?

Either way, I need this boy's name. Because if he and Jade were tight, he should have *some* answers. He could know why Jade McCall ran away and made up a whole-ass different persona. Or he might be able to tell me if she was in trouble and trying to hide from somebody or if something else weird was going on with her.

I flip back to the very first page. Focus on the pictures artfully placed inside square plastic pockets. In one relatively current shot, the pair pose in front of a Christmas tree inside what looks like a school gym decorated with silver streamers, snowflake cutouts, and fake snow. They wear matching reindeer pj's and Santa hats and touch the curved ends of candy canes together so they form a heart. When I slide the photo out of its holder, I find what I'm looking for on the back:

10th Grade Santa Bash!

Love you, J.

—Ryan

"Jade Bear, lasagna's ready!" I jump at Mr. McCall's voice and swivel toward the door. Beside it is a smart panel that I didn't notice before.

My stomach tightens at the necessity of more time spent pretending.

"Are you on your way?" he asks a minute later, his disembodied voice tinged with concern.

"Coming now!" I say to Mr. McCall, then realize he can't hear me. The speaker on the smart panel wouldn't automatically be broadcasting my response back.

I lay the photo and scrapbook on top of the desk. Then, as I'm shutting the desk drawer, something snags my gaze. LC always carries what she calls "brilliant white" drawing paper so she can capture whatever's caught her eye. A corner of similar paper, bearing the pencil shadings of a sketch, sticks out of an AP Chemistry textbook. The paper tugs free easily. I hold it between both hands and stare down at a woman's face. It's the face LC always draws—the face that LC claims is nobody but has always looked so familiar to me.

I trace the sketch outline with my finger. If the woman is important enough for LC to always draw, then maybe she's somebody else I can seek out. She could be a family member LC shares

more with than her parents, a favorite teacher, or a coach. I'm plac-
ing the drawing back inside the chem book when a crumpled sheet
of notebook paper that's folded in half falls out. I open it and read:

*Everybody hates me at Woodard. I wish I could just leave. Be
somebody new.*

I gawk at the sentences.

I wish I could just leave. Be somebody new.

Please tell me this shitty situation *did not* happen to me
because of Jade's school drama. Befriending me to hijack my life is
a seriously drastic solution.

No, my gut insists there must be more to it. Something more
sinister.

LC PACES MEGAN'S ROOM, the repetitive movement helping her focus on her most immediate problem: Megan's upcoming recital she's supposed to be practicing for. No, LC won't be able to be Megan forever, but while she's here, she needs to be believable. She can't have Megan's parents or sister asking questions. Not when LC has already listened in on the call where Megan begged Sophie to believe her about a body swap. Megan's parents might never jump off the cliff into the realm of impossible, but Sophie, whose head is always in some alternate-reality video-game world, just might.

This is going to hurt, but you're strong, and the pain will go away.

LC flinches at the memory of those words once spoken to her. The woman who uttered them was coaxing LC to be fearless—when LC should've been the opposite and fled far away.

Trusting the woman was one of LC's many mistakes.

Probably her biggest one. And now LC can't afford mistakes of any size.

Think, she demands of herself. *Fucking think. How to get out of the piano dilemma?*

Right when she's about to hurl a punch at the wall in frustration, a solution comes. She breaks out in a cold sweat merely imagining it. She hates what it means she'll have to endure. She is sick of trauma and anguish—in any form.

And she wants to throw up thinking about how her solution could irrevocably alter Megan's future. But there's no other way. She has to prioritize LC—place her own safety first, like she didn't do before. Injuries heal. Megan will be fine. Or at least LC tells herself that.

So, gathering her courage, LC turns toward Megan's closet. She opens the creaking door wide and braces one hand against the inside frame. With the other hand, she grips the door handle.

One . . . two . . . three!

She slams the door, stifling a scream as the pain explodes.

Eight

"Can I get a new phone and laptop?" I ask Jade's parents. We ate the lasagna mostly in silence, thankfully, and now they're sitting across from me at the backyard patio table, sipping sweet tea and exchanging comments about the "delightful" and "unseasonably warm" fall evening, as if everything is perfectly normal.

Their demeanor, given the situation, is bizarre. Yet not surprising. During spring semester of tenth grade, I participated in a cotillion season because it looked cool on episodes of *Gossip Girl* and *All American*, and I was going through my Serena van der Woodsen phase. Most of the teens were upper middle class, like my family; they also came with a side of hella bougie, unlike my family. A lot of them attended private schools, and their super-involved parents behaved like the McCalls. When anything upsetting happened with their kids—no matter how big—they'd pretend there wasn't a single thing awry. An asteroid could be on a collision course with Earth, and they'd continue tossing around carefree smiles and small talk.

Maybe the McCalls' power of denial helps explain how they missed something being so wrong with their daughter that she ran away.

"Excuse me. Sorry to interrupt, but did you hear my question?" I cut into the McCalls' meaningless conversation as respectfully as possible. "May I have a new phone and laptop?"

Jade's parents exchange a look.

Mrs. McCall turns a too-bright smile on me. "Eventually, yes."

Mr. McCall clears his throat. "We'd like to wait until your therapist approves it. We don't feel entirely comfortable with you being in touch with people."

"You understand, don't you?" Mrs. McCall says. "We don't know who you've been spending time with, or . . . who you might contact who may not be . . . good for you."

Beneath the table, my hands grip my seat cushion. Clearly, I have a mountain to climb before they start to bend on certain things. "What about friends coming over for visits while you're home?" I ask. "Is that a nope also?" Pretending I'm Jade with her friends might be even harder than with her parents, but I can't stay isolated if I want to dig up everything I can on her.

"Depends on the friend," Mr. McCall says, hedging.

"I was thinking of Ryan."

Mrs. McCall purses her lips as the two of them briefly look at each other. Mr. McCall threads his fingers through hers. "Let your mother and I discuss it more before we give an answer, okay?" he says to me.

"All right," I say, managing to keep most of the exasperation out of my pitch. "But I don't want to come home only to feel isolated," I add. "When you talk, can you decide on friends other than Ryan that I can hang out with too?"

I gather I said something right because Mr. McCall nods at me in the way parents do when they're pleased with their kid. "We can do that."

"I'm so glad to hear that you're looking forward to seeing people," Mrs. McCall says. She sounds somewhat surprised, which makes me think of the note I found in Jade's room about how everyone at school hated her.

"You do mean Woodard friends?" Mr. McCall says, his brows knitted. "Right?"

"Of course. I want things to be better this time around," I say, giving what I hope looks like an earnest smile.

"So do we," he says. "Phyllis made you red-velvet brownies—Aunt Vesha's special recipe—for dessert!" He nods to the plate in the center of the table—dark red squares with stripes of fudge icing sit atop it. "I figured it'd be a nice welcome home present. Not made by your aunt's pastry-chef hand, of course. But they should do for now, and Vesha is flying down from Chicago next month for Christmas to make them herself!"

I should probably eat one to keep building goodwill with Jade's parents, but I can't bring myself to do it. Out of all my reinventions—my jumps from friend group to friend group and interest to interest—being vegan is one identity I haven't just been trying out. Like piano, it's been fundamentally me since I was ten.

"I'd like to skip the brownies," I say as gently as possible. "I'm vegan now, remember? Brownies are usually made with eggs, which fall under the animal-products category for me."

Jade's father's hands tighten around his half-empty glass of sweet tea.

"I'm sorry," I add. "This change is super important to me, though."

"What brought this on? You used to love meat." Mr. McCall shakes his head, looking lost. "We scarfed down turkey legs during our annual Disney World visits. My Jade Bear loved red-velvet brownies, too!" Before I can respond, he abruptly pushes back from the table and walks with brusque steps into the house.

I stare after him, bewildered. Who gets that upset at their kid expressing a new food preference?

Caught off guard, I barely repress the flinch when Mrs. McCall reaches across the table and cups my cheek. "It's hard for him. It's hard for the both of us, feeling like we don't understand you the way we used to when we've always been so close. Not knowing why you left or what changed is terrifying. And now, again, you seem . . . different."

I tense up at her words, and at the probing expression in her eyes.

"Everyone goes through phases, right?" I say lightly. "I'm still me."

"I know. But it's been more than that, Jade. Even before you left. You know, your social life. The choices you were making . . ."

Before I can subtly find out what she means, Mr. McCall

emerges through the open sliding glass door and retakes his seat. "I apologize," he says. "I won't let my emotions get the better of me again. This isn't about me. It's about you—my kid." His words seem rehearsed. Like some perfect and acceptable response that's been fed to him by a therapist. Did he leave to go call someone to talk him through it?

Mrs. McCall grabs her husband's hand, squeezes it, then grabs mine, too. "This is a lot to handle for all of us. We're going to hit rocky patches. I think what's most important is that, as a family, we keep the lines of communication open. I want us to try being entirely open and honest about things that are bothering us. Can we do that?"

"Sure," I say, since it's what she wants to hear. I don't know what spurred this change in tactics, from pretending everything is fine to "being entirely open," but maybe it'll help me figure some things out—as long as the openness is on their side, not "Jade's."

Mr. McCall smiles faintly and says, "Okay."

"How about we start now?" Mrs. McCall says. "I'll go first. I want to ask you, Jade, about the goodbye note you left."

Mr. McCall clears his throat again, and he and his wife share another one of their looks. Mrs. McCall holds his gaze, adamant about whatever she's trying to convey.

I swallow. "What about it?"

"We've read it over and over, and it never made any sense," Mrs. McCall tells me. "We always wondered if you'd been forced to write the note—if you hadn't *really* run away, because it seemed *so* unlike you. We knew you were unhappy at school, and that the nasty social media drama between you and your friends last summer made you feel ostracized at Woodard this new school year, but still . . . you rarely make hasty decisions." Clear consternation creases her face for a moment before she smooths it. "Are you comfortable with telling us if leaving had something to do with Lai—"

"Let's just enjoy Jade's first evening home, please, without going there," Mr. McCall cuts her off. "Can we?"

Yes is what I should utter. But I can't drop things quite yet. Not when they've mentioned a message Jade left behind. "Can I see the note? Just to remind myself what I said—and to remind myself not to be that dramatic again."

"Why dig this all up?" Mr. McCall says.

"I don't see how it'll hurt," Mrs. McCall tells her husband. "It's good that Jade is reflecting on what happened and that she wants to reflect on it *with* us."

Eventually, he nods. "All right." I watch him walk through the kitchen and disappear into a closed room off the adjoining living space.

He returns with a piece of white paper and hands it to me. Finally, I'm holding what might be a tangible clue to start figuring out why Jade ran. The paper trembles a bit in my hands as I unfold it.

I read the typed, printed words.

Mom and Dad,
I love you. A lot. It's why I'm so sorry I have to leave.
But I need a fresh start. Don't waste time looking because

78

you'll never find me. I'd say not to worry, but I know you will. And I'm sorry about that too. I promise I'm safe. Move on with your lives without me, please.

Love, Jade

I want to laugh, cry, and scream at the same time. I see why the note frustrated Jade's parents; it doesn't explain a damn thing.

I suppose it *does* eliminate the possibility that she ran because of her parents. Otherwise, it makes no sense that she'd have bothered to write this. Not to mention, it had to be something bigger—something more abnormal—than problems at home or drama at school for her to have done something as fucked up as stealing my life.

Maybe . . . maybe if she has this weird, supernatural body-swapping ability, she was running from somebody who found out about it? That's usually how it works on TV. I hope I'm reaching, because if someone else knows—someone Jade was running away from—that means I might be in danger now, since I've assumed her identity.

"Thanks," I say, handing the note back to Jade's dad. I can tell they want me to say more, but I just give a small smile.

After dinner, the McCalls lock the patio door and rearm the house. While the three of us stand around the island inside the kitchen, they ask if I'm ready to head upstairs for bed. The two of them are clearly exhausted. Mr. McCall's gray eyes are tinged red, and Mrs. McCall stifles three yawns in a row.

"Get some rest," I tell them in the tone of a concerned daughter. "It's been an extreme day for everybody." The truth of the statement makes me realize how tired *I* am, and it's a fight not to show it. Instead, I feign alertness. "I'd like to stay up for a bit longer and enjoy being home. Maybe plop on the couch and find something on Netflix? Is that all right?"

They share one of their looks. I brace for the answer to be a firm no, but Mr. McCall beams. "I'm glad to hear something about my Jade Bear hasn't changed." He pulls me into a hug. "Do you want me to make you popcorn and grab you a soda? I can do tea or coffee too. Whatever you like."

"No," I say a little too quickly. "I'm good." I point in the general direction of the foyer and stairs. "I want my fantastic parents to go get some rest, because I feel terrible for everything I've put you through." I immediately want to smack myself because I sound fake as shit.

But Mrs. McCall's only response is a kiss to my forehead. "Okay. We'll give you some space," she says. "We're right upstairs if you need anything."

When the McCalls leave, I get comfortable on the brown leather couch, under a cashmere throw blanket. I kick off my shoes, tuck my feet beneath me, and play the first Netflix show that pops up in Jade's *Currently Watching* queue. I count the minutes that pass on the elegant gold wall clock.

One.

Two.

Three.

Four . . .

I let a full thirty minutes pass by. Then I turn off the TV and tiptoe to the room where Mr. McCall retrieved LC's goodbye note.

The door is slightly ajar. Giving a last look toward the staircase, I slip inside and quietly shut the door behind me. I feel for a wall switch and turn on the light, illuminating a home office—large desk, bookshelves, file cabinets. If the goodbye note was being kept here, there might be other stuff related to their daughter's disappearance. Maybe printouts of DMs, since they mentioned social media drama between Jade and school folks shortly before she ran away. I walk to the glossy ebony desk and scan its surface. Chrome laptop, glass paperweight, fancy ink penholder, framed family photo . . . all maddeningly banal, like the other things in the McCall household. My disappointment makes me realize that the sci-fi-loving part of me wildly hoped to find—*crap*, I don't know. A mad scientist's office? Something to explain how an ordinary teen girl has the ability to body swap!

My heart falls when I don't see a landline to try to reach LC at my house again, either. Of course I don't, though. I know like maybe three people who have an actual freaking house phone these days.

I open the laptop and confirm what I already guessed: it's password protected. *That's not what you're here for anyway*, I tell myself, trying not to feel discouraged. I'm looking, chiefly, for anything about Jade's disappearance, like the goodbye note. Stuff like that probably would be kept in a drawer, and I still have all of those to go through—two tall file cabinets with six drawers apiece. I notice that two of the drawers aren't quite closed all the way. I start with one of those, hoping maybe Mr. McCall left it open when getting the goodbye note. I riffle through the files as quick as possible, looking only at the tab labels: *Mortgage, IRA,*

Renovations . . . Nothing of use. I leave the drawer a bit open, exactly as it was, and move on to the next, biting the inside of my cheek hard enough for it to sting. When I open the second drawer, a current of excitement surges through me. One file is a little higher than the rest, as if someone recently looked through it. And the tab label says: *Jade.* The tips of my fingers tingle with excitement as I hold it. It's THICK.

"Jade?"

I jump at Mrs. McCall's voice. It doesn't sound close by, but it's hard to tell with the door closed.

My heart begins trying to hammer out of my chest. I shove Jade's file in the cabinet and rush from the room before Mrs. McCall can find me in it.

"You didn't answer the living room intercom when we checked on you," she calls as I ease the door shut behind me. She's nowhere in sight, and the acoustics of the open space make it hard to tell where she might be.

"I changed my mind about the snack! I'm in the kitchen!" I hurry through the living room. "I didn't hear you!"

Mrs. McCall steps into the dark kitchen from the other side of the room, a frown on her face. When she looks beyond me and in the direction of the office, it takes everything in me not to swivel around and double-check that I closed the door completely.

Shoot!

I remember too late Mr. McCall left it slightly ajar.

"I just got in here," I say weakly, and it sounds like bullshit. "Hadn't had a chance to turn on the lights. You really don't have to worry about me and hover," I add, forcing myself to cross the room and hug her. "I'm not going anywhere. Promise."

Jade's mom sniffles. When I let her go, she cups my cheek like she did at dinner. "I know I'm the parent and should be reassuring and supporting you in every way right now. But thank you, Jade. I really needed to hear that. Can I help you get your snack?"

"I've got it. Like I said, you don't need to hover. I'm not so fragile."

Mrs. McCall winces. "You're right. I'm headed back upstairs."

After she leaves, I busy myself getting a glass of water and a handful of chips, waiting to make sure she's staying upstairs before I return to the office. Finally, I gauge I'm safe and quietly hurry back. But when I try to turn the knob, it doesn't move. The door is clearly locked. There's a number pad above the handle. *Crap.* I'll need a code to get back in! I stab some obvious codes into the keypad—1234; 1111; 9876; 9999—before admitting it's a waste of time. The code likely isn't anything basic. I rub my head, thinking. Maybe the McCalls keep a list of codes and passwords somewhere; Mom and Dad do that. Or an events calendar with birthdays circled might help me? Tomorrow I'll try that.

I'm buzzing with too much anxious energy to go to bed or even to actually watch TV. I've *got* to keep doing *something—anything.* I decide to take advantage of the alone time and familiarize myself with the downstairs layout. As I step back into the living room, I catch a flash of a tiny red light blinking in a corner of the ceiling. A security sensor. I curse under my breath for not having considered possible indoor security cameras before as I squint at the little black square that the light shines from. I don't think I see anything that looks like a lens. So I hope for the best and go about my self-guided tour, reminding myself that even if there are security cameras, the feeds would only be checked after a break-in or something.

In addition to the rooms I've already been in, I discover the entry floor consists of a larger library with more floor-to-ceiling bookshelves; an indoor swimming pool (because the outside one must not be extravagant enough); a formal dining room complete with a china cabinet holding crystal dinnerware; two bathrooms; a pair of hall closets; and a game room that's just as massive as the rest of the rooms in the McCall family house.

I stand in the game room last, my eyes roving over a pool table, old-school *Donkey Kong* arcade game, air hockey table, and Yamaha keyboard. I cross to the keyboard, and it must be my frayed nerves, the compulsion to *keep* doing something rather than just stand idle, that makes me perch on the bench and brush fingers along the keys. Without thinking, I place my hands in the starting position for my showcase piece that I've been practicing since June. Immediately, I feel like *Megan*.

But the minute the first chord rings out, I come to my senses. The McCalls could easily hear if they're still awake. I can't explain away Jade suddenly becoming a classical pianist in three months.

Hold up. Maybe I should play. Because it would be bizarre. Maybe so bizarre that it'd convince the McCalls I am not their daughter if I tell them the truth.

No. That won't work. They'd commit me for sure.

I stand from the bench. Yet I can't bring myself to step away from the keyboard. The desire to continue playing, to continue being myself, is fierce. It's more than a *want*. It's a *need* that pulses through me with an intensity that leaves me aching.

I spy a pair of black studio-grade headphones hanging from a hook on the wall above the keyboard. I lift them off the wall and plug their cable in. I fit the cushions over my ears and sit back on the bench.

I fall into the concerto.

LC's fingers are slimmer and longer than my own, and I stumble at the beginning when I try to play with my usual intensity. The concerto sounds like trash. There's no smoothness to the piece. No fluidity connecting the individual notes. These hands aren't mine, and the muscle memory isn't there. I cease playing, flexing my hands on the keys, arms trembling and ready to just give up.

No. I try again—stubborn. I *want* to play. And I *will* play. Everything else has been ripped from me. But piano . . . This I can cling to. This I can have control over and retain some part of me even while trapped in this nightmare.

I adjust to the hands' different size and flexibility after a little while and start playing almost like myself. I let all the dread and anxiety ooze out for a short while. I hurl everything I've got into it—the love and the passion and the joy—like I do during recitals. I wrap myself in the protective, grounding, soothing comfort of the feel of speaking with music, of channeling it through my hands, of being *Megan*.

Nine

The McCalls escort me to Jade's first therapy appointment the next morning.

"I know this might be scary," says Mrs. McCall as we walk toward a gray-brick office building. "But it's a good step in the direction we want to keep going. And I'm proud of you for being here." She correctly reads my trepidation, even if she doesn't know the true source. I've never been to therapy before; I've never so much as talked to a school counselor one-on-one as *Megan*. How am I supposed to go pretending to be *someone else* and get it right? I already messed up while eating breakfast with the McCalls, not knowing who they were referring to when they mentioned someone named Keith, who turned out to be Jade's uncle. (Luckily, I was able to cover it up by saying my brain was foggy so early in the morning.)

We've made it to the sidewalk outside the therapist's office when Mrs. McCall says, alarmed, "Oh dear." Two teens are walking toward us: a white girl and a Black boy. I immediately recognize the Black guy, who wears army-green joggers and a *Spence Baseball* tee, as the one from Jade's pictures—Ryan. The scrapbook photo must've been snapped extremely recently because he looks nearly the same, including the waves in his hair and subtle swagger.

His eyes widen, and he stops short when he spies us.

"Hi!" I call out and silently urge him to come over. I'm not prepared for this, but I need to take the chance to connect, even briefly. A first step.

He stays frozen, as if he isn't sure if he should. The girl beside him gawks at me.

Mr. McCall gives Ryan a hearty wave. Ryan's brow furrows, but then he's heading toward us. I fidget with the sleeves of Jade's Spelman sweatshirt, wondering what exactly I should say to him.

The girl he's with follows close behind him, her arms crossed. Obviously, *she* isn't happy that Jade is back. Maybe she's one of the school friends Jade had issues with? I have no idea how Jade would act when confronting that situation, either. *Shit.*

"Good to see you, son!" Mr. McCall says enthusiastically as Ryan approaches.

"Gabe!" Mrs. McCall squeezes out through a smile that's all clenched teeth. "Don't encourage him. Now isn't the best time." Maybe she's right. But her protest—and my second thoughts—come too late.

"Jade?!" Ryan sputters in disbelief when he reaches us. He starts forward as if to hug me but then hesitates, shoving his hands into his pockets, awkward. "Wow . . . I'm just really . . . shocked. When did you get back? Are you okay?" His tone is difficult to read. A little stiff.

I nod. "Yeah, I'm fine. I just got home yesterday. Settling back in." I force a smile.

His brow furrows again, and his piercing brown-black eyes bore into me, as if searching for the truth.

I bite my cheek and try to wipe *any* emotion from my expression; I've got no clue what silent communication the real Jade might toss out to someone who potentially knows her secrets. I blink rapidly, sure I'm failing. It's much easier to control the words you say than it is to control what someone reads in your eyes.

A shadow crosses Ryan's face.

"Excuse us," Mrs. McCall says to them, "but we have to get going." The girl with strawberry-blond hair next to him skewers me with a glare. "Everything you did to him was messed-up, you know? And now you're back without telling him?"

"Sorry," I mumble, and wonder what the hell Jade did. If he and Jade fell out, it'll make talking to Ryan about anything deep a lot harder.

"Sorry?" the girl echoes in a snotty tone. "That's all you can say?"

"Jade has to leave," Mrs. McCall insists. This time, she doesn't feign niceties. She stabs the rude girl with a fierce glower of her own. "We're nearly late." She loops her arm through mine and tugs me toward New Horizons.

"Hold on," I say, without caring how the next thing will look or sound. "Can Ryan come by the house later today or tomorrow, *please*?" I beg the McCalls. "Will you do that?" I ask him. "I'd like to talk everything out. I'm sorry about it all, and I miss you."

After a beat, Ryan responds tonelessly, "I have practice."

"Every day? What about when you don't?"

"You need to respect how he feels; it's for good reason," snaps his friend. She tugs on Ryan's arm. "Let's go."

Ryan and I meet eyes one last time, and then he turns to leave.

A pressure expands in my chest as I walk away with the McCalls. I've been pinning my hopes on Ryan knowing something—even a small clue that'll unlock a piece of Jade's story. But it's not like I can force him to talk to me.

"I'm sure he was just surprised to see you," Mr. McCall says, patting me on the shoulder.

I nod and pull it together, sensing an opportunity that Ryan curving me has provided. "I should've called him to let him know I was back," I say, playing on Mr. McCall's sympathy. "Could I . . ." I look at Jade's father with what I hope is a plaintive expression. "Maybe we could talk about getting me a phone again, after the appointment? I just feel like I should call him, and maybe a couple other friends, so it doesn't seem like I'm avoiding them?"

The McCalls share one of their frequent looks. "We already told you we'd revisit it then," Mr. McCall says.

"But we're not making any promises," his wife adds.

"Okay," I say limply as we ascend the steps.

When Dr. Erika Larson, my therapist, greets us in New Horizons's lobby, I pray that things start going better for me today. I *need* her to believe Jade is stable and trustworthy. I try to ignore my jitters as I ease onto a couch in front of her, just the two of us in her office. She's a thirty-something Black woman with pretty shoulder-length faux locs, wearing a chic magenta pantsuit. She starts by giving me a similar spiel to the one Cherise did, about confidentiality and all that.

"We can navigate these sessions as slowly as you need," she says. "I want you to be able to relax here, Jade."

"I don't think that I can," I admit, deciding honesty about that, at least, won't hurt anything. Anybody seeing a therapist for the first time could find it hard to relax, feeling like they're under a microscope. Although . . . maybe she'll read something more grave into it? "I'm gonna try, though," I add.

She smiles. "It'll get easier—I promise. Why don't we begin with you telling me a little about yourself? Anything you'd like me to know or think is important."

This is really starting. I rub sweaty hands down the front of my jeans. No doubt, Mr. and Mrs. McCall have already given Dr. Larson detailed information about their daughter. I need to try not to say anything that might contradict them.

I swallow hard. "I like owls and the beach," I answer weakly, recalling the things I found in Jade's room. "I like vintage clothes too."

There's a twinge in my chest. *Megan* doesn't like any of those things. I've read too many *Demon Bird* volumes, so I can only think of owls as messengers from hell; beach sand gets stuck in unmentionable places; and designer *vintage* clothing screams "trying too hard to be snooty."

"Those are cool things to like," Dr. Larson says. "Do you have any favorite beaches?"

"Yeah, I do. Labadi Beach in Ghana is my favorite," I say, remembering the picture. But the new lie about who I am tastes like ash. None of the Allen family is crazy about the beach. Our vacations are usually trips to Orlando, to hit up Disney World and Universal Studios. We spend a day at Hollywood Studios, which includes Star Wars land, specifically to appease my geekery. And we always visit Islands of Adventure to check off Sophie's love of roller coasters that leave your heart in your throat. *Sophie . . . I miss that little troll.*

Dr. Larson smiles again. "Thank you for sharing that. So, before we go further, I wonder if you could tell me, in your own words, what's brought you to therapy? And what are you hoping to get out of it?"

My heartbeat kicks up. If she already knows the details, I can't begin to lie my way through. Yet I have to keep seeming eager and willing to do the work of therapy. "Being ostracized at school was hard," I say, deciding on the simplest thing I know is true. "It got to be too much. Now that I'm back, I just want to forget it all and start over, you know? Leave the social media mess behind me."

Dr. Larson scrawls something down on her iPad, then leans forward in her armchair. I stare at a patch of the beige carpet in the ensuing silence. "Would you like to elaborate on that?" she says eventually. "Fill me in a bit?"

"Did my parents tell you why I had trouble with folks at school?" I ask, to see what she knows.

"It's quite hard having rifts with friends, isn't it?" she responds, telling me nothing.

I try again. "It is. Especially with Ryan. Did my parents mention him?"

"Let's not worry about what your parents have said. I'd like to hear everything from you. What's your friendship with Ryan like?"

Great. "Well . . . Ryan, he was my close friend. But like you said, it's hard." She's obviously expecting me to continue, but I don't.

She must take my new silence to mean I'm struggling heavily with the Ryan situation, because she offers, "We can wait until a later session to discuss that, if you like."

"Thank you," I say, and don't need to fake my relief.

"Can we talk for a little about how you were feeling while away from home?" Dr. Larson asks. "Were you in Graysonville the whole time? These sessions are about you, and we go at whatever pace you set, but I would like you to try to open up today, even if only a little."

"I was in Graysonville all three months," I say, knowing that's true, at least. "I—I felt scared because I was so far away from home. I missed my parents, and I felt guilty for making them worry."

"How did you take care of yourself? Where did you stay? No judgment."

"I sold some designer clothes I took from home for cash. And I made some friends there and couch surfed between their houses."

I use a story that'll be easy enough for me to remember and that shouldn't raise any flags.

Dr. Larson scribbles again, then says, "I understand that you didn't come home on your own but were found by the police there. How has it felt to be home?"

"Wonderful," I reply quickly. "And relieving." Despite the confidentiality stuff, I assume she'll give the McCalls a recap of how Jade is feeling, generally, and want to be sure to seem settled. "I really am so happy to be back. And I'm so happy to be able to reconnect with the healthy parts of my life in Fairburn. I'm ready to put all the drama behind me. Running away was an immature mistake. I've learned a lot of lessons, and I have a much better sense of who I am now. Nobody can make me question it again." I say the last part adamantly so Dr. Larson is convinced.

She sets aside her iPad and looks at me intently. "Jade," she says, "I don't want you to feel like there are certain answers I'm looking for. All I want are your honest feelings so I can be of help in navigating them. Okay?"

Crap. "I *am* being honest," I say.

"Excellent." Dr. Larson smiles. "Just wanted you to know you can be as messy as you want in here. No need to neaten things up for me."

"Would it be okay to ask for some advice, then?" I say, figuring I might as well use that expectation of messiness to my advantage.

"Sure, you can. That's part of my job."

"I know I've broken the trust between me and my parents, and I want to fix it," I say. "How . . . how should I rebuild it if . . .

Well, if I'm being honest, part of the reason I ran away was because they're a little too controlling. I love them, but it's suffocating. I'm not a little kid. How do I get them to see that and ease up after doing what I did? I don't want to stress them out more, but I'm scared I can't take steps to get better if the problem remains. I . . . don't know how to tell them that. So, yeah. I figured I'd tell you, and maybe you can help."

"Those are very normal feelings," Dr. Larson says. "Two things you can do in this situation are to think about what might have led to you breaking your parents' trust in such a way and to consider how to regain it. Does that make sense?"

"Yes," I say. "Definitely. I'll do both of those things. But, like, in the meantime, I really want my phone back. I get why they took it, but it's going to be really lonely not being able to talk to anybody outside of my parents. Not the folks I had drama with. Other friends. If I need to prove I can be trusted with one, that's totally fine. I'll agree to stay off social media for good. I was relieved to be off it while I was away." I pause a second. "It's just hard to know how to prove I can be trusted with a phone when I don't *have* one."

Dr. Larson is quiet for a moment, like she's weighing my response. "A phone is a big decision. A big step for both you and your parents," she says at last. "What's most important is to work to reestablish trust and communication, both ways."

"Of course," I say, and try not to look frustrated as Dr. Larson suggests potential strategies to accomplish what she advises. Not long later, she tells me our session is up. When she walks me to the waiting room and asks Jade's parents if she can speak with them for a moment, all I can do is hope that my performance in there was as good as I needed it to be.

"So, how was it?" Mrs. McCall asks, twisting to look at me from the front passenger seat of the car. "Did you like her?"

"A lot," I say. "She was easy to talk to."

"I'm proud of you," Mr. McCall says. He winks at me in the rearview mirror from the driver seat. "And Mom and I are both sorry for any time we've been too intense about grades or swim or Yale plans or anything else. Everything is going to be better from here on out."

"You're seventeen, but I guess we've never stopped thinking of you as our baby," Mrs. McCall says. "Dad and I will make adjustments to start treating you more maturely. Sound good?"

"I appreciate it," I say. Seems like Dr. Larson gave them a good report! "Does that mean I get a phone?"

Jade's parents glance at each other. "We still need to give it more thought," her mother says. I feel my face crumple. "It isn't about us not trusting you," she adds. "It's about us wanting to protect you while you're finding your footing. Can you work with us and understand that?"

I understand that, but I still want to scream. I don't argue, though, knowing it won't get me anywhere.

When we return to the house, I shut myself away in Jade's bedroom and collapse onto the bed. It's a safe bet I'm not getting a phone anytime soon, *and* Ryan refuses to come over. Both of those plans seem to be fails. I press my fingers against my temples, close my eyes, and try to think of something else. What other ideas have I had? The file about Jade's disappearance. Right. I still need to get the code to the office. I sit up and look at the desk, remembering I saw an old academic planner in there. My parents always use my and Sophie's birthdays as their PINs. I head to the desk and see the chem textbook resting atop everything else. I take out the sketch of the woman again. It's a long shot, but there's still the possibility she's someone I can find and talk to about Jade; I have that unexplored avenue left, too. She might be a teacher, cheer coach, or swim coach. . . . I keep an eye out for any old yearbooks while I'm looking for the planner, but I don't find either.

"Jade! Can you come down for a sec?" Mr. McCall's voice comes over the intercom. I drag in a breath, take a minute to get it together. Then trudge downstairs.

This time, I'm unable to muster a chipper mood.

Mrs. McCall gives me a heartening smile, maybe noticing my low spirits.

"Dad and I talked more about a phone. We really don't want coming home to feel like prison, and it isn't good or helpful for you to feel as if you're being given punishments for running away, so we guess a phone will be okay. As long as clear agreements about usage are in place, we can see how it goes. Dad is headed out to get you a new one. You can have your laptop back, too." She watches me, clearly waiting to see my face light up in that way parents do when they know their kid is gonna be happy.

I don't disappoint. My whole face stretches into a wide, deliriously happy grin.

Mrs. McCall's own smile dims, her expression becoming a little more stern. "We have two things we'd like to be on the same page about. First: no social media whatsoever. Second: While we won't be overbearing and make lists of who you can and can't talk to, no contact with anyone who isn't a school friend here in Fairburn. That includes anyone in Graysonville."

"Yes! Yes! Whatever I have to do, I understand and it's a yes!" I'd agree to being fitted with a whole-ass ankle monitor—or brain chip—if it meant coming into possession of a device where I can finally contact LC again.

LC! (That's what you want me to call you, right? Not Jade?) It's Megan!

I'm at your house in Fairburn.

WTF! I mean seriously WTFFFFFFF?

How the hell did this happen? Please tell me we can undo it.

We really need to switch back. What if we end up stuck like this if we take too long to re-swap?

We need to come up with a plan to meet. If you're in trouble, and that's why you did it, I'll help you. We can make my folks believe the truth. They'll help too.

Text or call me back! ASAP!

I stare at the messages I desperately texted LC at my own number with my new phone. My first impulse was to curse LC the hell out. To tell her I didn't know what she had planned, but that I wasn't fucking living my life as *Jade*. But then I realized . . . if she did this because she's scared, and running from something, and if she has *any* feelings of friendship for me at all, I need to play on that. I need to get her to think that I'm on her side. That we're in this together, still besties.

Five minutes pass without any response. I want to kick myself for turning off the read receipts feature on my phone—the one LC is using. I was trying to be *enigmatic*. If I hadn't, I'd at least know if she's read my messages yet.

My heart slams against my rib cage as several more seconds drag by that feel like a thousand years. While I wait, I end up biting my nails—my extreme nerves making an old habit kick in. But then I think about the fact that I'm actually biting *someone else's* nails and freak out at how gross that is. I snatch my thumb from between my teeth, feeling a little ill. Clearly I'm spiraling because chewing Jade's nails is the least of my worries.

As I'm trying to rein it in, a message finally flashes onto the screen.

LC? I'm really sorry. My parents don't want me being in touch because of your troubles. And I still feel really weird from whatever drug you gave me. So this is the last you'll hear from me. Very very sorry. Good luck.

I blink and reread the text.

No. Oh fuck no. Oh hell no.

I reread the words again and again and again, somehow retaining enough awareness to know that if I shriek, the McCalls will come running. And moreover, if I start screaming, I'm afraid I won't ever stop.

What do you mean? I type frantically, hot tears rushing my eyes. **Why are you doing this? What's wrong with you? Tell me what you did! And how to undo it. I want my body back!**

I'm crying and shaking uncontrollably by the time I finish.

I realize I've been holding on to a naive hope that LC did this out of desperation. That as terrible as it was, as awful as she'd been, she'd agree to reverse it if I could talk to her, help her. I wanted to believe the girl I thought I was best friends with actually existed. But she doesn't. Nothing about her or about our relationship was real.

LC does not exist.

And Jade McCall? She's pure fucking evil.

WALKING "HOME" FROM SCHOOL, LC pockets Megan's phone. She's complete shit for the text she just sent and for ignoring the ones that follow. LC knows Megan won't give up. She might be naive and too trusting, but when Megan sets her mind to something, the girl is the most determined, laser-focused person LC has ever met. It's one of the things they have in common. She will keep at it. And if she eventually convinces somebody to listen . . .

LC wishes she could tell Megan the whole truth and just say, *If you play along for now, I'll find a way out for both of us! If you cause problems, it's going to be worse.* But it's too dangerous.

LC's gaze travels to the purple cast on her left hand. The fact that she needed to go to such lengths over piano lessons is proof of how focused Megan can be when she decides to see a thing through. If Megan hadn't been so dedicated to the instrument, there'd have been a less painful way out.

Getting through school has been savage, too. Thankfully, over the weeks they were friends, she asked Megan a ton of questions about classes, students, teachers, study habits, clubs, etc., so LC has managed. One of the reasons she chose both Megan and Jade was that they didn't have lots of close friends at school, which makes it easier.

The phone vibrates with yet another text. She yanks the phone from her pocket, but it isn't Megan. It's Nathan—the guy who threw the party—asking Megan out. LC's mood brightens.

She knows that it's just a silly distraction, wanting to spend time with him. But is it so terrible, wanting to have small things she's never enjoyed before, like a boyfriend, that make her feel like she's living a normal life?

Speaking of her "normal" life . . . she's just gotten to the Allens', and the first thing she does—which she does after every time she's been out of the house—is race upstairs. She goes to the closet, lifts the spare comforter, and checks to make sure the duffel bag with the cash and metal case is still there. She skips over the money and lifts the case with her good hand. She hates the case. Despises what's inside. It can't do anything other than wreak pain and devastation (two things she's had her fill of). But fear of losing her escape route forces her to routinely check that nothing has vanished.

When you lose enough precious things, it makes you paranoid. . . .

Despite everything you've taken from Megan, LC tells herself, *at least Megan still has all her memories.* She pulls a silk scarf—gold with red poppies blooming the length of the fabric—from the duffel and promises herself that someday she'll get answers and justice.

As soon as she can figure out how.

Ten

This is vile, Jade. 8:05 a.m.

You know this is serious, right? You're really hurting me. I'm scared. 8:05 a.m.

I miss my family that you STOLE from me. 8:06 a.m.

I want to go home, and you need to go home too. Like for real. 8:07 a.m.

Your parents love you. They've promised to be less controlling, and I believe them. If this is about jealousy, my parents won't be what you think. They're strict in their own way. I had to hide my piercing, remember? 8:09 a.m.

Or if you ran because someone here knows what you can do and threatened to tell, I'll help you deal with it. Was it a person at school? Is that the reason for your drama—somebody found out and thought you were a freak? You're not. Forget them. They don't matter. 8:10 a.m.

What the fuck, Jade?! You have to text me back. You can't do this. This is so wrong. It's twisted. 8:13 a.m.

I never get a response to any of the messages.

I'm on my own.

And Jade's trying to freaking gaslight me. Acting as if a body swap never happened!

Clutching the cell phone, I hug my knees to my chest in my bed. I haven't left my room since Mrs. McCall's voice on the intercom tugged me out of a fitful sleep, telling me it was time for breakfast. Thankfully, she indulged me and let me skip; there was no way I could face her, her husband, or any of the outside world without fracturing.

What will it matter now if I do? The depressing thought worms into my mind along with the whisper that I'm going to be trapped in LC's body forever. After all, what *can* I really do if she won't talk to me so I can convince her to change back?

I toss the covers off me, too warm, and leap to my feet. I pace back and forth, staring down at the unanswered messages and willing LC to just damn respond.

I want my life back.

I want Mom back, Dad back, Sophie back. Even the things I'd cut loose (like Ava) and the things I took for granted and that annoyed me (like living in boring Graysonville and only ever doing mainstream, unoriginal activities) feel like vital, precious pieces that I've lost and desperately want back.

Then find a way to take them back! A stronger voice eclipses the desolate one. It yanks me out of the bleak hole. *You will not give up! LC is awful, but fight back. Fix this yourself. Find a way to expose her and make people believe you're telling the truth. Or figure out how to reverse this yourself! There's got to be a way.*

It's like a law of the universe: *For every action, there's an equal and opposite reaction.* Body swapping isn't part of the physics curriculum Dad teaches at my high school, but that principle has to hold true no matter what, right?

I sit at the desk, pull up a private search browser on the laptop, and type: How would a person swap bodies with another person?

Dozens of articles immediately come up. And it's not just a slew of conspiracy blogs. The search results include legitimate articles. Some virtual simulations have even been conducted to see how swapping might affect someone's psyche and alter their sense of self. That's where the hard science published on the topic ends. Other scholarly essays present two prevailing theories for how swaps could occur: one is a total brain transplant, and the other posits that the brain isn't where a person's essence is stored. The latter group believes that such an independent consciousness— your soul, perhaps—is what would need to be swapped, and occult practices are the only way to achieve it. I chew on the second theory, since Jade obviously didn't perform brain surgery on me in Nathan's backyard. Of course, mystical shit means I'd need to reverse some creepy magical charm. Wild as that thought is, I can't just dismiss the possibility. At this point, Jade possessing supernatural powers is as plausible as anything else. What she did to me was way outside the realm of the ordinary.

I search a new phrase: Real-life accounts of body swapping.

It gives me a mix of the same articles about virtual experiments, blogs about mysticism that don't look remotely credible, and wikis of fictional worlds that body swapping occurs in. I scroll through page after page, and none of the 126 hits are of any use.

Then I look up one more search term: Sci-fi shows with body-swapping explanations that make sense. One thing I know well is hard-core fandom culture. People get mad serious about what they like and get hella angry when they think creators fuck it up, and they love to post their opinions. That means there will be Reddit threads complaining about sci-fi shows that don't explain the science behind swapping well enough and others praising shows that do.

I come across a thread on this show called *Immortal Futures*. I haven't watched it, since I prefer soft sci-fi, but the posters rave about how eerily possible it is for ports to be installed in humans that make it possible to upload our consciousness to a computer and then download it to a brand-new body. The processes described, though, are too intricate for Jade to have performed undetected at a house party while I was blacked out.

Exiting the browser, I give myself a pep talk. *I can still try to get Jade's file.*

If I'm able to get a second look at it, maybe I'll uncover concrete info about her life before she left that'll help me.

* * *

I finally find the planner I saw in Jade's desk; it's wedged into the back of a drawer. But when I look through it, there's nothing written in it at all—no scribbled reminders of family birthdays that might be the door code. Throughout the day, whenever the McCalls aren't downstairs, I try punching in random number combinations, but even after what seems like a thousand different tries, the lock doesn't budge. Then when I'm passing through the kitchen, I notice a wall calendar hanging discreetly beside the fridge. After a quick glance around, to make sure I'm alone, I quickly flip through. Yes! Birthdays and the McCalls' wedding anniversary are written down. I grab a pen and scribble the dates on my hand. Rush back to the office and press each date into the keypad in turn, and . . .

. . . the lock still won't open.

I want to smash my fist against the door.

But I can't afford to give in to frustration. If I can't see the file, I've got to make Ryan talk to me. At this point, I'm not even quite sure what I'm hoping to find out from him. But a best friend since childhood definitely would have sensed something strange going on with Jade. In my room, I pull up Ryan's number on my phone and type a long apology text, mostly about how shitty it was that I hadn't immediately told him I was back.

Ryan replies almost immediately. That's big of you. Are you ok being home? For real?

Honestly, I write back, I'm struggling a bit. I'd feel better if we can hang and talk. I'm in therapy, but it's lonely being home. I feel like I have nobody outside my parents. Are you sure there's nothing I can say to get you to come over?

Afterward, there's a moment where I experience a prick of guilt for playing on any sympathy he has for Jade. But I've got no other choice.

I can come today. Ryan's response turns guilt into excitement.

Are you busy right now? I type back.

Not really. I'll head over. See you soon, J.

Ryan and I hang out by the firepit, just the two of us. I'm grateful for our alone time, and astonished Mr. and Mrs. McCall let it happen by going out to run errands. Mom and Dad would never. Whenever I have guy friends over, even just school project dates, one of them always plays chaperone.

At first, we sit in silence. I know I need to talk to him, but for the moment, the silence feels right. The only sound is a soft susurration of wind as the late-afternoon sun sets. I steal a moment to appreciate how much I love fall evenings and the crispness I can smell in the air. When I was little, me and my best friend, Sasha, used to hang in my backyard around a firepit during this time of year and roast marshmallows until they were gooey, a little burnt, and delicious. We'd never want the graham crackers or Hershey's bar that went with s'mores. Only the giant marshmallows.

"What are you thinking about?"

It's the first thing Ryan's said to me after the reserved "hey" he offered at the front door.

"Nothing," I say, turning toward him. I can't utter the truth—that I'm thinking about my past and the friendship I miss—perhaps the only one that ever felt one-hundred-percent right until LC came along. Ava and I were close, but she didn't all the time *get me*, get me. She didn't understand how we could be besties but how I also wanted to chill with other friends that she wasn't feeling. Or how I could be obsessed with fan conventions and drag her to a Noize Crew show and scream my head off. With her, I always felt like I had to pick one or the other.

"Nothing?" Ryan says, brow furrowing. "You kept things from me before, too. You know? Like how bad things with your old crew were. And who you were becoming at Woodard and outside of school." He pauses. "I mean, we've always been close, right? Did that change and I missed it? I know I'd gotten crazy busy with baseball, but I could've been there for you more if you'd let me."

"I'm sorry, Ryan," I say. "Um, when exactly did you start feeling that way? A long time ago? Or . . . did you think I got really secretive only right before I left?"

Ryan gives me a look, as if it's a silly question. "Since last spring, when you started hanging with ya new girl and ditching plans all the time."

I flash back to Mrs. McCall mentioning the changes to Jade's social life. "Yeah . . . my parents aren't such fans of her either." If this friendship is part of what Mrs. McCall meant, it could be that the friend got Jade into something wild.

Ryan shakes his head. "My bad. I shouldn't have mentioned it. Your parents asked me not to talk about her with you."

I don't want to push too hard. I'm supposed to be smoothing things over. "All right. We don't have to talk about her, then," I say. "But can you tell me other stuff I started doing that irked you? I'd like to clear the air about everything."

"It doesn't matter," Ryan says quietly. "I'm a jerk for bringing it up in the first place. I was upset with you. Hella upset. You ran away and ghosted everyone for months. I mean, you have no idea how worried I was. But I shouldn't have started unloading. You're dealing with your own things and don't need more drama." He runs a hand across his low-cut hair. "Let's just forget about it. All I want is for you to trust me this time so you don't get to the point where you're lying to everybody, tripping out on drugs, and picking up crappy, random friends who don't care about you." He touches my elbow gently. "*I* do care about you. That's the only real reason I'm mad. I don't want to see you out of control like you were before or in a spiral that makes you run away again."

Okay, now we're getting somewhere. I nod. "I can do that." The mention of drugs makes me think about the Molly Jade had at Nathan's party and how stoked she was to do it. According to Ryan, her interest in drugs was new. I wonder . . . did she start doing them, keeping secrets, and pulling away from old friends because she was hiding something way huger than Ryan could ever conceive of? And if she had a new friend she kept ditching him for, did the friend know her secret? If so, that means this friend is someone else out there who knows body swapping is real, and she could know how it's done.

"Have you seen the shitty friend around since I left?" I ask Ryan casually, with a hint of a joking smile.

"Uh, if you're not doing so well, maybe we should switch to happier stuff now?" Ryan says.

Ugh. "Sure," I say. "Tell me what I've missed?" I can get more info about Jade's life in Fairburn Heights, if nothing else.

For the first time, Ryan looks amused. "Oh, so you think you can just roll back and I'll spill all the tea?"

"Yup," I say, returning the grin. "That's exactly what I think."

He launches into telling me all about the beginning of the "epic junior year" that he and Jade had been looking forward to since eighth grade: an annual back-to-school upperclassmen-only lake party; a Starry Night homecoming dance Jade served on the planning committee for last year; a fall carnival where Ryan used his killer throwing arm to dunk some boy named Will (apparently Jade's jerk ex) as repayment for cheating on Jade with a Woodard friend.

"*Will* . . . ," I say. "Do you think there'll be any drama when I go back to school over him and what happened?"

Ryan scowls. "No. I'll make sure Will isn't an ass."

"Are you sure? There isn't *anyone* I'll need to worry about?" I phrase it like Ryan should already know who I've got in mind and like I want him to admit I'm not tripping.

He scowls harder. "Such stupid shit popped off because of Will's lies. But your entire Woodard crew felt terrible after you ran away. I think everybody who took his side is sorry and will be happy you're back too."

"That's good to hear," I say. The note Jade wrote about wanting to disappear was probably because of this boy and his drama—not caused by a school friend potentially finding out about her horrific abilities.

"Regardless, *I* want you here, J," Ryan says, pulling me out of my thoughts. "I was so worried about you, and *I'm* glad you're back. I know I was kind of an ass yesterday, but I was in shock. You've been my best friend since we were in diapers, and nothing changes that. Okay? You'll always have me. There's no need to feel lonely."

"Thank you," I mutter awkwardly. Ryan gives off the vibe of a good guy—an amazing guy—who lost his best friend. I hate it for him that this is all bogus.

I have to focus on the positive, though—at least I have a new lead after talking to him, this friend of Jade's that nobody likes. And if I keep rebuilding the relationship with Ryan, I should be able to get a name out of him.

He stays only a little longer, catching me up on some stuff with his family and asking how it's been with my parents. ("It's been weird," I say. Understatement of the year.) I walk him to the door when he has to go.

After he's gone, I'm about to head upstairs. But when I see the McCalls' maid, Emma, putting on her coat to leave for the day, an idea hits me.

"Excuse me?" I say to her. "Could I ask a quick favor?"

"Yes, Miss?"

I glance back at the glass door to make sure I don't see the

McCalls' headlights approaching, then say, "I can't find my phone. I'm pretty sure I left it in my dad's office, but I forgot the door code. Can you give it to me?"

The older woman frowns, her blue eyes narrowing with uncertainty.

I quickly add, "Whenever my parents leave, they're strict about me keeping my phone near and answering when they call to check-in. They'll be really mad if they've been trying to reach me." I smile in a pained way to try to play on her sympathy.

She chuckles in understanding. "I have the same rule for my kids. I'll let you in." I want to whoop in relief when she agrees. After all that hassle trying to figure out the code, this is all it took!

After the maid punches in the door code and says goodbye for the night, I move as fast as possible—quickly finding the file, opening it on the desk, flipping through pages, one after the next. I don't want to risk taking it out of the office, in case I can't get back in to replace it. I look over the pages, quickly but thoroughly. Most seem to be reports of false leads regarding Jade's disappearance and whereabouts: spotted on a bus to California, outside a movie theater, eating in the food court at the mall . . . Hope sinks as one page after another is more of the same. But then, a page near the end is the initial missing person report. I scan it, heart racing. My eyes trip over a part in the *Reporting Person's Narrative* section.

The McCalls said they suspect a new friend of their daughter's might have convinced Jade to behave out of character. They reported this friend to be a teen girl named Lainey Carter, who, according to the McCalls, was picked up by the police two weeks prior and found to have been lying about her identity.

When I read the name, goose bumps pimple my skin.

Lainey Carter.

This must be Jade's new friend nobody wants to speak about. The friend that she ditched Ryan for.

LC. Lainey Carter.

If Jade also had a friend named LC . . . did Jade just name herself after her when she ran to Graysonville? Or . . . The blood drains to my feet. If this LC girl who everyone thought was a bad influence changed Jade in such crazy ways . . . maybe I didn't actually ever know Jade, herself. Maybe LC—whoever she is—swapped bodies with Jade first.

Maybe the person I knew was Lainey Carter *inside* Jade McCall's body.

Eleven

Lainey Carter.

I scroll down the Google search on my laptop, which hasn't returned one hit for a Lainey Carter around my age, including no arrest records. All I've seen are public social media profiles for a handful of adults and a couple of obituaries from many years ago. After being so energized by having an actual lead to follow, I'm now overwhelmed by frustration again. I need to find out who LC really is. She's got to be a third girl, separate from Jade; it's the only answer that makes sense. And I need to uncover how and why she's targeting folks repeatedly. The fact that she's *collecting* victims . . . The real Lainey Carter is more of a monster than I imagined.

What's her endgame? Could it all be some sick, twisted experiment to hurt people and ruin their lives?

My stomach clenches, a startling realization hitting me. LC can't possibly fake being me forever, and she didn't pretend to be

Jade for long. So . . . when she's done trying to be Megan, for whatever reason, she'll do what she did before. Run away to another city and take my body with her and ditch it when she swaps with someone new! And if LC *keeps* swapping bodies, it's gonna become impossible to find her. At some point, she'll be completely out of my reach, and I—and everyone else she jacks—will be stuck.

Panic balloons inside me. The police found Jade, but it took three months. What if nobody ever finds "Megan" after LC runs again? And I can't even imagine how traumatized my family would be if they thought I'd run away.

I want to cry.

I've never hated myself more for being so dumb. So easily duped.

Somehow, though, I don't give in to the impulse to cry. Instead, I focus on controlling what I can and doing what I can to save myself.

I text Ryan and ask if he wants to hang out again, so I can pry more about Lainey from him. Maybe I can make it seem like it'll be good for me somehow. . . .

The phone chirps a few seconds after I message him.

That's cool. I don't have practice tomorrow. I can come over after school.

It's getting boring around here. Can we chill away from the house? I ask. Ryan might be more relaxed about the topic away from here.

Does Adventure Quest for 3pm sound good? Are you still into that? It'll be fun and should help shake the funk.

I have no clue what Adventure Quest is, but if it's something Jade was into, I should probably agree.

Can't wait to see you! I type back. Let's kick this funk!

I really should have googled "Adventure Quest."

I stare up at the treetop obstacle course towering way too damn high above the ground. I'm terrified of rope courses. Freshman year, our class visited a similar place on a field trip. The majority of my classmates had a blast. I tried to be fearless alongside them. I put on the safety harness and helmet and clipped into the course on the launch platform and everything. I took five courageous steps onto the skinniest of wires, glanced down, imagined some freak *Final Destination* accident happening with my harness and my guts splattering all over the ground—and lost my shit. It was mortifying. I was stuck on the wire with a line of my classmates griping at me to move out of the way already. In the end, one of the course guides had to coax me to the nearest exit platform and then help me climb down the side via wooden planks nailed to the tree that almost gave me a heart attack too.

I got ribbed the rest of the field trip and the bus ride home. I wasn't aware I even had a fear of heights until that day, since I love roller coasters. But being inside a metal car and walking on my own along a sliver-thin wire dozens of feet in the air are *not* the same thing.

Let's pick a different activity, I almost plead to Ryan as we step up to the brown-haired girl staffing the ticket counter. Jade likes this place, sure. But a girl can develop a new fear of heights. Right?

Suck it up, Megan, I tell myself. *Just get through this. Faking it has been your strategy all along. Keep doing it. More info on Lainey is what matters.*

"Would you like entry for two hours, three, or five?" the park worker asks.

"Two," I say before Ryan can answer. Even if I am going forward, there's no need for overkill.

Ryan raises an eyebrow. "We usually go big or go home."

I wince. Of course jumping headlong into five freaking hours clipped into the trees is their usual.

I shrug and keep my voice casual. "I'm out of practice." I don't need to "fake it" here to produce a convincing, nervous laugh. "So let's start off small? Don't want to waste money."

"Your total is $71.42," the park worker tells us.

"Since when does the bad and bougie Jade McCall care about wasting money?" Ryan cracks, handing over his credit card.

I pop my lips, attempting to keep up the easy banter. "Ha ha. I'm only trying to be a good friend and not run your pockets."

Ryan grins widely, and I get a little stuck on it. The boy *is* gorgeous.

I shake my head, shattering the spell because I absolutely should not be thinking of how cute he is in these circumstances. "Let's hit that course," I say, spinning toward the safety harnesses that are laid out on the ground a few feet away.

I never get the chance for air to fully return to my lungs. Less than ten minutes later, after a brief safety refresher for repeat climbers that only heightens my anxiety, I stand on a platform nestled high in the canopy of giant oak trees. Above me is a wire that I'm attached to by my safety harness. And below me . . . is hard earth.

"I'm afraid," I cop to Ryan, not making the same mistake I did freshman year and waiting until I'm steps away from the platform to chicken out. I grip the rope attaching my harness to the wire so tight my hands sting. "I know the old me did this all the time," I say. "However, the new me—"

"It's okay, J," he says quickly. He slings an arm around my shoulders, squeezing me in a sideways hug. "No need to explain. You were . . . away for a while, and I'm sure went through a lot. Wanna unclip and just . . . I don't know. Talk again? We can go get smoothies or something else?"

Yes. Right now. GET ME OUT OF THIS TREE! It's what I should yell if I have a scrap of good sense. But a disappointed look crosses his face. It really is adorable. And I'm apparently a sucker for it. More importantly, though, these types of activities are supposed to help with cementing bonds and trust between people. Which is the ultimate reason I boss up.

"It's cool," I say. "I'll stick it out. Can we . . . stay together, though?"

"Are you sure?" The caring way he says it and the concerned glint in his intense brown eyes make it clear that if I said otherwise, we'd leave right away, no further questions asked. He really is a great guy—and a good friend to Jade. Most other friends would pester me to tough it out, like Ressa Thompson (one of the popular girls I wanted to impress in ninth grade) did during the field trip that ended in disaster. Trying to fit in with her and her crew was how I ended up clipped to a wire in the first place, when I knew I should've stayed on the ground with Ava, who encouraged me to keep it parked from the moment I looked up in the trees and gulped down air.

"Yes. I'm positive," I say, making the decision to prove something to *myself* this time, instead of to someone else. I want to show myself that I do have the guts it takes to get my life back. It's silly and the tree course has nothing to do with the body swap, but somehow it feels like it does.

"All right. Whatever you want," Ryan says hesitantly. "We can't step off the platform at the same time, so do you want to go first or have me go first?"

"You," I answer quickly.

He gives me a salute as if I'm a drill sergeant. It'd be corny on any other boy and I'd roll my eyes. But with Ryan, I giggle. When he moves in front of me to lead us off the platform, my eyes stray to his butt, which is really cute in his jeans.

Stop it, I order my hormones. This isn't a real date. Or anything like it. This is only me needing to stay in proximity to Ryan for information purposes.

Ryan takes three steps onto the cable before turning back to me and holding out his hand.

I look down at the ground that seems to sink farther away. My mind seizes the exact moment to paint a picture of how my *Final Destination* freak accident will occur. My rope will snap away from my harness. I'll break my neck. And my back. And my skull. And I'll be in excruciating pain, if I don't die immediately. Plus, if I do die in Jade's body, does that mean my mind dies too? Like permanently? That's the catch to body jumping in a lot of movies. Or will I be this weird, disembodied ghostly presence without a host? *Oh my God*, how would I ever get back to my own body then?!

"You look like you're going to be sick," Ryan says. "This was a terrible idea. We can—"

"I'm okay."

"Don't look at the ground. Use me. Stare right here."

Following his advice, I train my eyes on him and force my feet to move off the platform. I yelp preemptively, anticipating a wobble that never comes. When I did this as Megan before, my sense of balance on the wire was like my rhythm: nonexistent. But apparently, muscle memory is a real thing, because Jade's lithe, athletic body handles itself like an expert on the wire. The moment I leave the platform, my center of gravity shifts to stabilize me, my calves and toes flex to help with balancing, and my body weight redistributes itself perfectly. I want to yelp again, but this time in triumph.

Until I realize something that stops me cold. I'm becoming used to Jade's body. Getting way too comfortable with the way it moves and how its muscles react to stimuli and how tall it is and how limber it is. Will I become used to Jade in other ways and separate more and more from who Megan is?

I do wobble then, dizzy with the frightening thought.

"I got you." Ryan reaches out to steady me. His movement throws me against him. His arms lock tight around my torso, clutching me to him. My heart beats in my throat—and not because I almost slipped off the wire.

It's only after someone on the platform behind us clears his throat that I realize how we must look. My entire body blazes. "Uhhh . . . sorry?" I sputter.

Ryan releases me, stays by my side, threads our hands together, and promises, "I won't let you go until we're back on the ground."

I somehow manage to complete the course despite my new worry. However, as I walk the wire, climb through a barrel that sways alarmingly, and hop between swinging discs with ease, it is clear that getting details about Lainey is more imperative than ever, before I lose myself in ways I never conceived. In fact, when Ryan asks if I want to go a second time, I can't do much except stare up at the course that I conquered and wonder in horror: Did I even prove Megan's bravery up there, like I wanted to? Or was it Jade's abilities that did all the work?

Twelve

"Soooo, I don't want to make things awkward," I say to Ryan as I casually stir a straw around my berry smoothie. "But my therapist wants me to try out this strategy where I confront things that are nagging me head-on instead of letting them fester."

"Oh. Okay," responds Ryan, sounding concerned. He's seated across from me at a small circular table in Juice Land, a smoothie chain that Jade apparently loves. I nixed the idea of a second go on the ropes course, so we came here instead. "Are you . . . mad at me for something?" he asks.

"No!" I assure him. "You've been incredible. Way more forgiving than I deserve. This is actually about . . . Lainey." I keep my eyes on my smoothie as I talk. "I know I made my own decisions with the drugs, but Lainey was super into that scene. I can't stop worrying about her, and it's making it hard to concentrate on what's important: my recovery. I get she's not good to be around and I'm not going to seek her out," I say, to make it clear. "But can you please tell me if anything happened with her while I was gone?

Have you heard what she's been up to? Or who she's hanging with now? I only want to know if she's all right."

"Sorry. I haven't heard anything since the arrest," Ryan says briskly.

"So, you didn't see her around Fairburn at all after it happened?" I press.

He blows out a heavy breath. "I'm sorry, J. But no, we aren't doing this. Your parents asked me not to talk about her with you. And I agree with them. You probably won't want to hear this, but we've never lied to or bullshitted each other. LC is toxic, and she doesn't deserve your concern when she didn't give a shit about you. Please, forget about her."

LC.

I fidget with my straw, trying to stay calm.

Lainey Carter was also known as *LC*! So, this clinches it—Jade's friend named Lainey and the LC I knew are the same person for sure. I've never even met the real Jade McCall.

"We don't bullshit each other, remember?" I say, using Ryan's words against him. "Let me make decisions about what I can handle for myself, okay? What's your whole beef with LC? Is it only the drugs? Or is there something about her that I missed by being too wrapped up in our friendship? I don't want to repeat my mistakes."

Ryan studies me for a long minute. I draw myself up tall, try to reflect an inner toughness. "You've got points," he says. "And you do seem different. Stronger than when you left."

Different. He's got no idea. And "stronger" is laughable—last night in bed I started thinking about my family and cried my eyes out. I've been like two seconds away from cracking entirely since my parents banned me from the house.

"I am," I say.

He nods, then looks down at the table. "So, one reason I don't like LC personally: I think your friendship with her damaged you in some way, and she had something to do with why you ran away. I never really believed the drama involving Will was enough to make you do it. It hurt you, but when we talked about it, you told me he and the girls harassing you could fuck off. So I figure you must have left because of LC. She talked you into doing shit that wasn't *you* all the time."

"What did I do that 'wasn't me'?" I ask.

"You *hate* raves, Jade. But you let her drag you to them. Remember how gross you felt after that big one? And what about that nape piercing she convinced you to get? You missed a huge state-qualifier meet because you had to let yours heal. It was *states*, Jade. A friend who isn't shitty and cares about your college swim dreams would've suggested you wait until off-season."

It's a gut punch, listening to him point out the ways LC was a horrible friend to Jade and seeing the similarities with my relationship to her. Yes, *I* took the Molly (or what I *thought* was Molly) and drank at Nathan's party, knowing I had piano early in the morning and that every lesson leading up to the showcase counts. But LC did give me a push; if the situation were reversed, I definitely would've told her to take it easy. Which should've been a glaring red flag that something was off with my supposed best friend. . . . But I was focused on trying to at least appear like I could keep up with her.

125

And did I *really* want the piercing, or did I get it for the same reason I took the Molly? I finger Jade's barbell and laugh shakily. "Yeah. This was a stupid idea," I say.

"I sort of get it," Ryan says. "The one LC has looks cool. But I could tell you were just doing it to be like her. Not to be like *you*."

It takes a moment for me to register the significance of his words. When I do, my breath catches. He's saying LC talked Jade into *matching* piercings. Like she did with me.

Which means her original body, before she hopped into Jade's, had a piercing, too!

As I fidget with the small, seemingly innocuous barbell, I remember a theory on the Reddit thread about upload and download ports. And something new occurs to me: people in *The Matrix* had freaky neck plugs below the base of their skulls that functioned exactly like a port. The location of my nape piercing is almost identical to those plugs. What if the piercing is a port? And that port can somehow be used to access the mind, to transport thoughts between physical bodies?

That has to be how it's done! It's too fucking coincidental that the three of us have the piercings—*and* that Lainey suggested them to both me and Jade. This is more than just a possible clue! It could be a real answer to how LC did this—finally.

That "bonding" session in my room was her prepping me so she could steal my body.

My gut twists as I remember Sophie barging in on us, asking for a piercing too. If I'd caved . . . or been a more chill big sister . . . *Oh God*. And now LC is living in my house with her. Sophie doesn't give up on stuff easily. What if she asks for a piercing again? Rationally, I know it doesn't make much sense for LC to swap with someone inside my house, much less a little kid. But still . . . knowing someone as evil as LC is right there with Sophie, and that she has this ability—what if there's some other way she could use it to hurt Soph?

"Are you okay?" Ryan asks, cutting into my fear.

I inwardly wince because I have no idea what might've shown on my face, and I need him to keep trusting that talking about LC is *good* for Jade.

"Yeah," I say, hoping I don't sound shaky. "I'm just going to run to the bathroom real quick."

Once I'm in the bathroom, I splash cold water on my face to help me calm down. I've gotta go to LC and confront her in person immediately! Force her out of my house, get her away from Sophie, and make her swap back with me. If the piercing *is* an upload/download port, then I've got the proof of the technology that makes swapping possible literally embedded in my skin. I can tell LC if she doesn't switch and leave my family alone, I'll show the piercing to the police and tell them what it does. Who knows if the police would actually listen. But hopefully, the bluff will be enough to make her do what I want.

Having an actual plan—the start of one, at least—makes me feel less rattled. I pat my face dry with a paper towel and head back to the table.

"You good?" Ryan asks.

Hell no. "Yeah. I'm good," I lie. I stare across the table at Ryan, who's so supportive and kind and compassionate. It all makes me suddenly want to trust him, so bad, with my story. And to explain that LC has harmed his friend, too. The real Jade is out there somewhere trapped in a similar hell. Maybe she's being forced to live with Lainey's family and pretend, too? But I don't want to drive Ryan away while I still need him. Why would he readily believe something so wild, after all? Especially when he's so concerned about Jade's mental health.

No, better to keep the truth to myself, since I can't be sure how he'll react. I can lean on him for help in other ways, though, I think.

Hoping my gut is right, I say, "I know this is a big ask, but would you be open to driving me back to Graysonville?" I can't take myself since I don't have a car. "It's nothing crazy," I add, in response to his worried look. "Our talk about what it means to be a real friend just made me realize there's a girl I'd like to see, for closure. I'm asking you to go with me because I'd like you by my side, and because I'd like to keep it on the low from my parents so they don't freak. And if they do find out, it'll help if they know you came. They trust you."

A beat passes where I have no sense of what he's thinking. "So . . . just a quick visit?" he finally says. "I take you and bring you back right after?"

I nod. "Yup. Just one conversation. I'd really rather do it in person than over the phone."

"Could I be there with you when you see her?" he says. "Not, you know, listening, if you need privacy. But can I be somewhere nearby?" I open my mouth to respond, but before I can, he cuts in: "You can't expect me to feel okay about taking you when I don't know anything about this girl. It was some serious shit, you disappearing. And the whole reason your parents trust me is that they know I've got your back—that I'm not going to let you do anything stupid."

"I know," I say. "And I don't mean to put you in a spot. You can totally hang close by and keep an eye on me while I'm with her. Sit across the street, whatever. I won't disappear. I promise." I feel awful, knowing that the girl he's so protective of isn't even me. But if I can get through to LC, it'll be good for the real Jade, too.

He holds my gaze. "All right," he says. "I'll take you."

The shock must color my face, because he leans across the table and squeezes my shoulders. He gazes at me thoughtfully, his striking brown eyes glinting as if he's glimpsing something he didn't expect. "I would've said no to the Jade who left, out of worry. But you really do seem different. You're more introspective and honest with your feelings, and if this will help you keep going in that direction, I've got your back." He drops his hands but stays pitched forward. "What happened to you while you were away?" he asks softly. "Why do you need to talk to this girl in Graysonville so bad? Is there . . . a specific reason you can't just forget about her?" His voice gets gentler. "Did she mess with you somehow?"

His question hits super close to the truth. "A lot of stuff happened," I say, "and this girl was a solid friend when I needed one. She helped me, and I want to thank her and not make her think I ghosted her." It's a vague reply. To make it hopefully be enough so he doesn't change his mind about driving me, I add, "I'll be able to explain more after we go to Graysonville. I promise."

LC FINGERS THE SILK scarf with poppies splattered across it like blood. After she's used it to get the information she needs, she rests it next to her on the bed.

Frantically, with her uninjured hand, she scribbles in a notebook, recording the images that appeared in front of her eyes while she held the scarf: *In car. Black Volvo. State Street Bank next to Hillside Diner.*

When she's finished, she rubs the back of her neck, index finger running across the piercing. She flinches, like she does every time she hazards to touch it. The research lab and its owner take shape in her mind.

"I know that the methods I'm going to use to help you will seem unusual, but you've had an unusual life," Dr. Tess says. "Together, though, we're going to make things better for you," she vows right before the flash of pain tears through the nape of LC's neck.

Sitting here on Megan's bed, LC can't help herself from reliving what came next: Tess hooking her up to a computer; Tess assuring her that the missing memories weren't gone forever; Tess promising, "They're now stored outside of your mind, that's all."

LC bites the inside of her cheek so the pain can keep her firmly planted in the present. But she can't push the bad stuff away.

Tess still has those memories that she stole. Memories that include everything LC knew of her parents. Her entire childhood. Will she ever get them back? It's one of the reasons LC hasn't run farther. She can't quite bring herself to face the possibility of never reclaiming her past, and the farther she runs, the more out of reach it seems.

She roughly wipes her eyes as the door opens. Sophie stomps inside.

"I don't like Nathan," Sophie announces. "He has the intellectual depth of a puddle. You should dump him."

LC snaps the notebook shut. "I like him; that's all that matters."

Sophie's hands fly to her hips. Her eyes narrow on LC in an unnerving way. "What the heck is wrong with you? Why are you always so weird now?" Sophie looks at the cast on LC's hand pointedly. "Like, for real, though. You should be a lot more miserable about your hand and zero piano. Are you that wrapped up in this stupid boy?"

LC tries to smile brightly the way Megan does, making you

feel like you're in sunshine. "Nothing's wrong. I'm just stoked about my first real boyfriend. That's as important as piano to me right now. You'll get what I mean soon, Soph."

Megan's little sister skewers her with a look. "If that is what's going on with you, then you sound like the dumb one." She turns around and stomps away.

Afterward, LC remains on the bed, frozen, for a long time, thinking: maybe she should go farther away—California or something—forget trying to retrieve her memories. Sophie is too smart; she already suspects something is up. And Tess, who is hunting her and got too close in Fairburn, is so dangerous. If it comes down to it, any eventual confrontation will end with Tess winning. She always wins.

LC rushes to the closet and opens the case with the Cogitec materials, seeing what she already knew she would. Enough equipment for one more swap. That's it.

If she uses it and runs, instead of figuring out how to stay and make things right, won't that mean Tess has won anyway? Not only will LC not have her memories; she'll be stranding Jade and Megan in this hell.

LC wants to put herself first. She feels she deserves that, after everything she's been through. But is there a way to do it without permanently ruining other lives?

Only one more swap.

It's not enough.

Maybe Tess has already won.

Thirteen

"Park here."

Ryan does as I ask and parallel parks in front of Hyped Up, across the street from Graysonville High.

As we wait for dismissal, I studiously avoid letting my gaze stray to the coffee shop. Seeing its signature orange booths and starship mural on the wall through the windows is too freaking disturbing. Hyped Up is more than where LC and I first met—it was our special chill spot on lazy weekend days. We likely would've hung out there most days after school, too, if LC didn't supposedly travel an hour into the city each day to attend her midtown art school.

There are still so many things I don't know about how and why this all went down between us. Was she planning to jack my body that very first day we met? Did we even really meet by accident? Or did she target me? See something in me that assured her I'd be an easy mark? My hands clench into fists. Whatever she *thinks* I am, she's got another thing coming.

"You good?" Ryan asks.

I nod. "Just anxious about seeing the girl I mentioned."

"Is this going to be a . . . tense reunion?" He reaches over the leather armrest of his Jeep Wrangler and squeezes my left hand. His thumb draws soothing circles along the back of my skin until I unclench my fists.

I exhale a breath, surprised by how much his gesture helps. "Thanks," I say. "It'll be intense, but I'll deal."

"Remember, I've got your back." He and I are facing each other, and he leans toward me, lightly touching his forehead to mine. "For real. I got you."

I swallow—no longer even thinking much about LC. My mind has turned to imagining that the strands of my hair brushing against the side of Ryan's face aren't silky straight and black. I imagine they're violet and curly with kinky brown-black roots. I imagine Ryan is looking at *me*, Megan, this intently.

Get it together, I snap at myself. *He doesn't know you. He isn't looking at* Megan *in that endearing way. He's looking at Jade McCall. Plus, now is not remotely the time.*

Graysonville High's dismissal bell rings, slicing through the awkward silence that's settled between Ryan and me.

I look through my open window and take in the mob of students pouring out of the school. I ignore the ones rushing toward the bus lanes, student parking lot, and car rider line and instead scan the smaller group collecting at the crosswalk in front of the school. If LC is impersonating me, then she'll walk to Hyped Up for a Strawberry Crumble Frap, which is my usual routine.

After the buses pull out, Mr. Davis, our crossing guard, halts traffic and waves the walkers forward. It feels eerie to see kids I know passing by. I have the delirious thought that I could do literally anything right now—stick my head out the window and cuss out somebody, punch someone in the face, run across campus in my underwear . . . None of it would matter because I'm in someone else's body. A weird, unsettling freedom crashes over me from knowing that. On some level, it's intoxicating. I clutch the door handle to—

I'm not sure what I'm about to do. Nor do I ever figure it out. Because LC appears at the crosswalk.

My violet curls are hanging loose down her shoulders, and she's wearing my favorite thigh-high gray flat boots that lace up the back. She has on the purple *Black Geek Girl* sweatshirt I made on Tee-Nation freshman year, then decided was too dorky to wear to school. I sit here, staring, frozen in place as I watch. I'm seeing me but not me. The experience is surreal. Mind-boggling—like what folks who claim to have out-of-body experiences must feel, I imagine. Like I'm an Alice who has tumbled down a swirling vortex and is staring at her evil doppelgänger. I'm so freaked out that it takes me a minute to notice something: there's a purple cast covering my left hand and lower arm. "What the fuck did she do?!" I explode, forgetting Ryan's beside me. He sputters some startled response, but I don't process it. How *dare* she do something to my hand!

Ressa Thompson joins LC at the crosswalk. She's a part of my popular crew, but somebody who *I* keep my distance from. She and LC, however, are laughing together, LC looking as if she has no cares in the world. As if she isn't a thief who stole my entire damn life. When Mr. Davis motions for them to cross the street, LC hooks her arm around Ressa as if they're besties—like LC and I did together all the time when walking places.

She's replaced me. And with her.

The thought is a dropkick to the stomach. But the hurt is irrational—none of our friendship was real—and only lasts for a nanosecond, replaced by a surge of anger. First: LC being all buddy-buddy with Ressa Thompson is insulting to *my* character. Ressa's two-faced to legit everyone, a wannabe mean girl and bully, and I cannot stand those kind of shady people. Second: Hell fucking no. LC does not get to so easily and blissfully slip into my life like this, wear my stuff, go to my school, rob me of my family when I've been experiencing hell since Nathan's party.

"Wait here," I tell Ryan, and bolt from the car.

I run to where LC and Ressa stand—on our side of the street, under the crosswalk sign. My heart thunders when I reach them, my mind still struggling to truly process the moment. Looking at myself is unbearably, freakishly weird.

"Why?" I spit at LC. "What the hell is wrong with you?!"

She blinks at me and contorts my stolen face with convincing shock and confusion. "Why are you here?" she says. "Me and my parents told you to leave me alone."

I vibrate with fury. "They're *my* parents! Why are you pretending to be me?!"

Ressa makes a choking noise, and I remember she's there. "We need to talk alone," I tell LC. I reach for her hand to pull her off to the side. But she jerks away.

"I'm not going anywhere with you! You're clearly nuts."

"I know you swapped us on purpose," I say, no longer caring who's around since she won't do this in private. "I know you did it to Jade, too, and I know *how* you did it. The piercing, right?" She stares at me blankly. "Where is Jade? Come clean about everything, make it right, and I won't go to the police, tell them what I've figured out and show them my piercing. You keep running to avoid getting caught, I'm assuming. Well, there's proof embedded in the back of my neck and your neck." Her blank expression fuels my anger. "If I convince the police—or a doctor—to examine the piercing closely, are you afraid of what they'll discover, LC? Seems to me like you might be."

"What . . . what are you talking about?" LC says, and she really is a good liar. Because, *oh my God*, she even sounds scared—of me. She takes a step back as if I'm intimidating, and her arm tightens around Ressa, who's looking gleeful at the drama going down, albeit hella confused too.

"Stop!" I shout. "Stop faking shit! I know the truth, *Lainey Carter*."

Upon hearing her full name, LC pales. She looks like she's about to be sick. I narrow my eyes. "Are you about to puke because you've been caught? Or because you know you're a monster?"

"I don't know what the hell you're talking about, *LC*," she snaps.

"My name isn't LC, and you know it." I jab a finger at the purple *Black Geek Girl* sweatshirt she's wearing. "Just like *my* fucking sweatshirt isn't yours, and you know that, too. Neither are my boots, my school, my bedroom, any of my stuff, or my family!"

For a second, I swear she flinches. But in the next moment she says, "I'm calling my parents. My dad told you what would happen after Nathan's party if you kept bothering me. You want the cops involved? Fine." She goes so far as to take out her phone and let her thumb hover over *Dad* on the screen. "He's right inside the school," she says, as if I don't know that.

I clench my hands, and LC's smug grin dials up my rage. I've never been quick to violence before. I've certainly never gotten into physical fights. But I imagine hurling my fist into LC's face. I don't, only because it's *my* face. Still, I shove her hard against the light post.

The breath rushes out of her in an *"oomph"* that gives me immense, petty satisfaction.

"See?! You're insane! Get off me!" LC pushes me with the hand that's not in a cast.

As I stumble back, I grab at her sweatshirt and a strange vertigo hits me. LC and the sidewalk lurch. Pain ripples through my stomach. I double over, fighting nausea.

Disconcerting images flash in front of my eyes. In an out-of-body sort of way, I see Jade's body—the body that I'm in—bent over, clutching my stomach. It's as if I'm looking at myself doing it. Then, I see an image of Ressa, standing to my right—as if she's *next* to me, not in front of me. It's like I've leapt from Jade's body to reoccupy my own, real body, like I'm seeing out of my own eyes, not out of Jade's.

I close my eyes to steady myself and shake off the weirdness. A splitting headache has detonated inside my skull. A moment later, I jump at a firm touch against my elbow. Ryan. He must've seen the altercation. I reach for him without thinking.

His hold tightens. "What the hell is going on?" Before I can think how to answer, he turns his gaze to LC. "I don't know who you are, and I don't care. Me and Jade are leaving."

"You sure you want to get back in a car with that girl?" LC laughs. "She's got problems. Her assaulting me should've made that fucking obvious. And next time she touches me, I *will* call the police."

Fourteen

Ryan leads me back to the Jeep, his arms locked around me the entire way. I crane my neck to see LC still standing by the light post. I glare to let her know this isn't over; I'm not concerned about the cops. She's bluffing, the same as I was. She's got too much to hide.

I swear a guilty look crosses her face. But it's gone a heartbeat later, and she wraps her arms around herself like she's the victim. A white Mustang pulls up beside her. Nathan Ross pokes his head out the window, calls out hi, and LC climbs inside the car. I stare after it as it zooms down the street, remembering how hard she pushed for *me* to get with Nathan instead of going after him herself. A fresh wave of fury roils through me. It's sickening how she plotted and manipulated things.

"Come on," Ryan says quietly, urging me the rest of the way to the car.

As he's opening the door for me, Ava runs up to us.

I just stare at her, tired; I've got no spoons left to deal with another thing.

She braces a hand on the car's door and forces it closed. "I saw what happened between you and Megan," she says to me. "Leave her alone. Who the fuck attacks somebody like that?"

"We're trying to go," Ryan sighs, and I hate the way he looks from Ava to me, like he never should have agreed to drive me here. And Ava is looking at me like I'm toxic garbage—which I feel like I am, after hearing her defend "Megan" like that, despite how I've treated her in the past.

"Fine, go," Ava says to him, dropping her hand from the car. "But you should know, your friend is a cruel, sadistic bitch."

"Who the hell are you to—" Ryan starts.

"Who the hell are *you*—"

"Stop!" I say. "Please. Just . . . stop. I need both of you to listen to me!"

They turn at my outburst.

Without stopping to think, I tell them everything. The whole story, start to finish—rushing through it without a pause, not giving them a chance to interrupt and tell me I'm insane. Telling them may be a terrible idea, but I can't bear pretending for one minute longer.

"I know this all sounds crazy," I say when I'm done. "But I *am* Megan. Not Jade McCall. *Or* LC." I reach for Ava's hand but think better of it. "It's really me, Aves," I plead. "The other half to our Geek Girls Duo. Not LC."

"Now I understand," Ryan says, sounding angry. "Of course

coming here was about LC! You linked back up with her after you ran away, didn't you? She was here with you in Graysonville. Is this . . . some kind of twisted game she's got you playing? She made up this whole crazy story for you to tell us? Is she close by somewhere, watching this?" Frowning, he looks around.

"She isn't here," I tell him. "And I wasn't lying. I told you the *truth*!"

Ryan clenches his jaw. "J, you've gotta stop letting her trash your life."

"Please," I beg. "Please believe me. I'm not Jade!"

He hesitates. "You're scaring me now," he says. "It's time to call your parents. Your therapist too."

"No!" I shout. "No," I say more calmly, checking myself. "Please don't call any of them. It'll make things worse." I turn to Ava. "Ask me literally anything about our past," I beg her. "Make it something Megan would never in a million years tell LC or anybody else."

Ava grips the straps of her backpack. "You said something similar in the shed," she whispers. "And Freddy . . . Freddy never likes strangers much. But he couldn't get enough of you. It was like he already knew you." She shakes her head, like she can't believe what she's entertaining. She holds my gaze and asks, "Freshman year when we went to Dragoncon, what was your costume malfunction?"

I'm so happy, I want to cry and hug her at the same time. "We didn't do anime characters that year," I answer. "We pestered your grams to help us sew Marvel cosplays. I was Gamora. You were Nebula. Except you weren't the obnoxious version from the

MCU who told Star-Lord at the worst possible time that Thanos sacrificed Gamora to achieve the Soul Stone. You were the immensely better comics version. But that's not what you asked," I hurry to say, realizing I've veered offtrack. "I had a bad reaction to my green face paint, and my skin turned strawberry red and patchy. I ended up walking around Dragoncon looking like a humanoid reptile shifter. You tried to make me feel better by calling it a wardrobe malfunction and saying every great cosplayer experienced a blip at least once in their con circuits." I remember it worked, too. I wore my Snake Woman patches with pride and giggled with Ava about it all of Labor Day weekend. Mortification didn't set in until I went back and looked at the photos we took once the con was over. Then I decided I looked ridiculous and like a loser, and I deleted them.

Ava crosses her arms over her chest. "Which con did we travel to out of state?"

"That's a trick question," I say. "We never made it to one. Our parents wouldn't drive us that far or let us go alone. But we planned for senior year to be the year we convinced them, since we'd be turning eighteen. New York Comic Con—if we could score badges—was gonna be our big trip before we had to leave for college. But then—" I abruptly stop, cringing at what comes next.

Ava says it for me. "But then you dropped me when you decided I was too dorky and you wanted to distance yourself from the fangirl stuff you thought was too *uncool* and immature."

"I'm sorry," I say hoarsely, and mean it.

"You should be," Ava says. "It was triflin'."

"I—" I startle. Hope swells. "Does that mean you believe me, if you just tossed me attitude like I really am Megan?"

Ava grips her backpack straps tighter. "I don't know. Maybe?" She cocks her head to the side, peering at me intently. "This *is* the second time you've made the claim about a body swap. It's impossible to believe it's happening in real life. But . . . it's also impossible to NOT believe—because a firm principle of sci-fi, I guess, is employing science that *could* become real in the future. Maybe that future in real life is here? Hell. *Fucking-damn-shit!*"

Ava cursing means I'm really getting through to her, because she virtually never curses unless she's either super upset or awe-struck. I try to temper my hope, though. "Megan has been acting strange. . . . ," she says slowly. "She broke her hand, which is weird. You, I mean Megan, would never do that. She's extremely careful about not injuring her hands. And with the showcase coming, she would've been extra, extra careful about avoiding accidents."

That's why LC's wearing a cast! What if she did irreparable nerve damage to my hand? "You have to believe me!" I cry to Ava, growing frantic at the possibility of losing my ability to play per-manently. "I need help. I have to expose LC and find a way back to my body before she does worse damage! She hurt my hand, on purpose, to get out of lessons! I cannot lose piano or the showcase if she decides to do something more drastic!"

Ava pulls me into a hug. "I believe you. Only Megan would get this worked up over the showcase. You've been dreaming of an invitation since fifth grade."

I go limp in her hold, fighting back tears of relief. Somebody finally believes me. Somebody finally *sees* me.

"It's okay," she says. "We're going to fix this."

"How?" I croak. "If LC forcibly swapped bodies with me, how do I make her swap back if she isn't willing?"

"I don't know," Ava says, still hugging me. "But we will. I promise."

I grimace. "That's what I keep telling myself, yet . . ."

"Hold up! Wait. Wait. Wait," says Ryan, who'd fallen silent. He looks between us like we've grown second heads. "This *is* insane."

Ava steps back from me and regards Ryan with suspicion. "Who are you again?"

He holds up his hands. "I'm Jade's best friend. Which . . ." He laughs nervously, shuffling his feet. "You're telling me you aren't Jade? Really?" he asks me. Disbelief lingers in his tone, but now he scrutinizes me in a way that says he's considering the possibility. "You have been different. Super different," he says. "So, let's say I believe you. . . . If this is real . . . then where's . . . where's *Jade*?!" He stares at me like I have the answer. "What did LC do to her?"

"I don't know," I say gently. "If everything I'm guessing is right, she's a victim in this too. Wherever she is, she's in Lainey Carter's body." I reach out to supportively squeeze his arm. "I want my life back so bad. I'm sure Jade does too. There's got to be a way to achieve that for us both."

Ryan still appears to be in utter shock. "How?" he says.

"We know Lainey Carter was arrested, right?" I say. "I tried to look up public records of her arrest, but I must've been using the wrong search terms or something because I couldn't find anything. But still seems to me that's the lead we follow." I look between the two of them. "Will y'all help me track her down?" I ask.

Ryan doesn't respond. Just stands before me, horror-stricken.

"I'll do whatever you need," Ava says.

"Really?"

"Of course!" she says. "If this is all . . . real, *of course* I want to help you. But also, do you think I'd give up a chance to be part of a wild story like this? Body swapping! In real life!"

I smile. It's true—this is just the sort of thing she'd be fascinated by. "Thank you," I breathe. "I'm so sorry. You didn't deserve how terrible of a friend I was to you."

"I would hold a grudge," Ava says, hands on her hips, "but it looks like Lady Karma already taught you a lesson."

I sputter a laugh. Only Ava would say that in the moment. My ex–best friend is a dork, but she sticks up for herself. It's one thing I've always admired about her.

My phone vibrates against my leg with a text as I'm chuckling. I fish it out of my pocket. The message is from LC.

You need to stay away and live your life. Anything else is dangerous, and not because of me.

"WHAT'S WRONG?" NATHAN asks. "You've seemed off since I picked you up." The innocent question spears LC like an accusation.

"Nothing," she mutters, stuffing her phone in the sweatshirt's pocket.

"Whatever it is, I can make it better." Nathan's voice is low. Coaxing. Temptation personified. If any of this were her real life, a thrill would run through LC. She'd lean into the cute boy and do something as normal as initiate the kiss he's angling for.

Instead, she turns away and gazes up at Megan's house that they're parked beside. She still feels the full brunt of Megan's anger, and worse, the hurt and betrayal that bled from her every word.

"Thanks for the ride. I've got to go," she tells Nathan thickly, without turning his way. She clambers out of the car, shutting the door soundly behind her. She doesn't deserve to enjoy stolen kisses with a boy after school. She doesn't deserve the house she's walking toward or the family who lives here, either. All she can think of is how she's done Megan a heinous violence.

And the worst thing of it is, what she texted to Megan is true. No matter what damage LC has done, Tess is the bigger danger. Eventually Tess will figure out that "Jade" is back home, and then Megan will be in danger from her, too. And of course, that's LC's fault.

When LC escaped from Tess and swapped bodies with Jade, everything happened so quickly. It needed to happen quickly: Tess was right on LC's trail, able to track her body no matter where she went. LC was almost delirious with fear, and her "friendship" with Jade had been a whirlwind. With Megan, though, there had been more time—all that time they spent together. Even though both girls were innocent, and she hurt them so terribly, she felt more guilty about Megan. The bond with her felt real.

LC can't just ignore the harm she's caused this time, no matter how hard she's tried.

As LC unlocks the Allens' front door, the feeling that she's an intruder hits her yet again. She hears Mrs. Allen's voice from inside and pulls out her key. She can't do it. Can't pretend right then.

Instead, she remains outside and sits on the porch swing.

LC's thoughts turn to her own first encounter with Tess. She can still remember her desperation, living on the streets at fifteen, having run from foster care. She wasn't proud of what she had to do to survive—picking pockets, stealing food, conning people . . . Then one day she targeted the wrong person: a white woman in her late twenties, sporting an expensive-looking pantsuit. LC figured some rich lady wouldn't miss the cash she lifted. Tess caught LC stealing her wallet, but instead of calling the cops, she offered LC a place to stay. LC was skeptical, no doubt. And she should've held on to that gut feeling. But she went along with it because the choice was that or having no warm shelter during days that were already turning cold.

Tess was so nice at first. She promised LC that she would have a home and somebody to look after her for as long as she wanted. Tess told LC she was a therapist and offered to help her heal from "the trauma of a difficult childhood" after she noticed the burn scar on LC's arm, a reminder of how a foster mom used to punish her. Tess seemed to be the first person since her parents to actually give a shit. And she was a doctor. So LC believed she really could make things better. Grateful, LC let her guard down, was hopeful about the therapy sessions, and started thinking of Tess's place as a permanent home.

But nothing that seems too good to be true actually is. It was a lesson she'd learned in foster care and again on the streets. She should've stuck to her number one rule: trust nobody to look out for LC except LC.

"I have access to very advanced technology," Tess said. "I can adjust your thoughts and emotions with technology far more precise than any drugs. I can do amazing things for you, if you keep an open mind and trust me. You'll be a part of something experimental but innovative and life-changing for a lot of folks," she added to make LC feel special for once in her abysmal life— and it worked.

LC shakes the memories out of her head. She can't keep reliving them. Doing so makes her weak. Afraid. Makes her feel like that fucking gullible, trapped girl Tess was able to prey on.

Once more, she thinks of Megan and the fight she saw in her today. It's a fight LC wishes she herself had had from the very start when Tess finally revealed her true nature and intentions. If she'd gotten away sooner, Tess wouldn't have had the chance to wipe LC's memories.

LC is so damn tired of running and hurting others to stay safe, though. For a second, she allows herself to envision being more like Megan and having the courage to confront her monster head-on.

Does LC have that courage? Ever since her memories were stolen, she's been plagued by the thought that she doesn't know herself anymore. How can she truly know who she is inside if she doesn't know where she comes from? And if she doesn't know who she is, how does she figure it out?

Fifteen

"Okay. I think I've processed," says Ryan, after we've sat quietly in his Jeep for a good length of time. I turn from the window; I've been staring at my school, lost in thought. Among other things, I've been thinking about Ava and how lucky I am we saw her. Aside from helping search for any info on Lainey Carter, she agreed to keep an eye on LC at school—to keep track of who she's hanging out with, stuff like that. And to try to touch base with Sophie, too. Just to make sure she's okay.

I wait for Ryan to continue, knowing how heavy of a bomb I've dropped. If he's coming around, he'll need to do it in his own way, at his own speed.

Another minute crawls by before he speaks again. "The girl you called LC—the one you had a fight with—isn't someone I've ever seen. And you're saying . . . that the body she's in is . . ."

"Mine," I say. "It's mine. My real name is Megan Allen."

Ryan nods slowly. "And that Ava girl, she first thought you

were LC, because Lainey Carter hung out here in Jade's body? Am I getting this right?"

"I know it's confusing," I say. "But yeah, that's right."

"And Ava knows you well."

"She was my best friend a while back."

"You convinced her of all this," he says. "With all that friend history stuff. And, like I've said, you've definitely been different— I mean, Jade's been different—since getting back. Like, even looking into your eyes is different. Hard to explain."

We hold each other's gaze for a moment, and I wonder what he's seeing in me. "So . . . you believe me?" I ask.

He hesitates, and then says, "Crazy. But I guess I do."

A weight eases from my shoulders when he says it. I've got two people on my side! Two people who know and believe the truth! *Thank God.* I'm so glad to hear that," I say. Things would've become infinitely more difficult if Ryan returned to Fairburn and told Jade's parents she was having a mental breakdown.

"I have a question," Ryan says, and grabs his phone out of the cupholder. He scrolls to a pic of Jade and another girl showing off their nape piercings. Their backs are turned to the camera, so I can only see the second girl's profile. But she's a little taller than Jade, skinnier, and her complexion is a medium brown. Her hair is a reddish brown that she wears in the same short, sleek bob that I'm wearing. In the photo, Jade's hair hasn't been cut yet. "Do you know that other girl?" Ryan asks. "Have you ever seen her?"

"No," I answer. "I'm guessing that's the real Lainey Carter."

"Yeah," he says hoarsely. "I have to find Jade. I have to help her."

"We will," I say. "We just need to have faith." I keep my voice even and try to at least sound like I have enough confidence for us both. In truth, I feel so in over my head. Each day I spend as Jade leaves me more petrified that I won't be able to get myself out of this. And now I need to help save the real Jade too? I don't know if I can do any of it.

"Shit." Ryan's curse pulls me out of my own head.

I blink at the strange way he's now staring at me. "What's the matter?"

"I'm such a douche," he says. "I've made this entirely about Jade, and you've had the same fucked-up thing happen to you too. I'm sorry."

"You have nothing to apologize for," I say. "Of course you're worried about your best friend. Besides, I'm not the one who has vanished. Jade *is* missing. And if she's inside LC's real body, she might be in danger." I fidget with my phone in my lap, thinking about LC's message.

You need to stay away and live your life. Anything else is danger-ous, and not because of me.

I show the message to Ryan, and say, "LC could be making this up, to frighten me, but I've thought about the possibility before that she's running from somebody."

Ryan stiffens. "We *have* to find Jade ASAP."

"About that," I say slowly, deciding on a plan I can't believe I'm about to propose. "I know this could be a bad move for folks like us, but I don't think we have any option other than the police. We can't tell them about the body swaps, obviously. But we can go to Fairburn's precinct and ask if Lainey Carter is still in jail after her arrest. If she's not, we can ask who she was released into the custody of, since she's under eighteen. I'm not sure how we're going to convince the police to give a couple of random kids info on where Lainey Carter is, though. Let's pray we get lucky?"

"I've got an idea that's better than luck!" Ryan says, mood lifting. "My coach's wife is on the force. I can ask her directly; she loves me and might do me a favor if I tell her it's important I talk to Lainey for some reason. I can ask Coach when she's working, and we can go see her when we get home."

Hope fills me, even as his use of the word *home* in reference to Fairburn Heights causes a pang in my rib cage.

I press a hand against my chest, and as I do, I catch a flash of violet out of the corner of my eye. I glance down and see a purple hair on my yellow sweater. The curly strand, from my real body, must have landed there during my scuffle with LC. Seeing the reminder of what was stolen makes the hurt in my chest crack wide open.

"Are you okay?"

I don't answer Ryan. Instead, I pluck the purple strand off my sweater and hold it carefully, irrationally not wanting to lose the scrap of myself.

As I pinch the hair between my thumb and finger, I'm suddenly hit by a wave of dizziness—the world tilts exactly as it did when I fought with LC. The onslaught of vertigo is as swift and vicious.

Images bombard me, flashing in front of my eyes in a rapid succession. I see my front porch. My legs dangling from the swing. Mom's flowers in the garden . . .

What in the hell?!

I fumble to roll down the window, mash the button, and inhale fresh air. Maybe this is some sort of panic attack? The dizziness doesn't go away. Neither do the images of my porch. I see Mom's potted ferns. A string of kids getting off a bus at the corner. Sophie's among them.

It's like I'm in two places at once, like I'm both in this body and in my real body.

A headache kicks up.

"I don't feel well," I tell Ryan.

I open the door and lurch forward, the nausea growing. I clamber out of the car and empty the contents of my stomach onto the asphalt. I slap my hands against my knees, shuddering. Hands tighten around my shoulders. Ryan's. My face heats. How long has he been standing behind me? *Oh my God.*

"I'm sorry," I say.

Ryan hands me a bottle of water. "Drink this. It'll help." He unscrews the top and tips the rim to my lips. I swallow small sips—he's right, it helps. The images have stopped and the world is stable again. The nausea has receded.

Back in the car, I try to explain what happened—the visions I saw of the outside my home, both when I pushed LC and when I held the violet hair. It's hard to put into words. The description of it sounds ridiculous to my own ears.

"We're going to get you and Jade free of this mess," Ryan says, laying a hand on top of mine. "I know it's a hell of a lot easier said than done, but going to the precinct should be a solid start." His voice now carries a reassuring conviction. And I'm so, so thankful not to be alone in this nightmare anymore.

When I'm back in Jade's bedroom, by myself, I summon the courage to touch the violet hair again. I might be reaching, making connections where there are none, but I want to test out a theory. I slip the hair from the pocket of my jeans, and as I hold it, the vertigo hits again. This time, I'm prepared for it.

I glimpse the inside of my bedroom—my real bedroom. It's not a continuous vision, just flashes of isolated images: the fuzzy star pillow I keep on my bed; my most prized manga and comic volumes on the bookshelf nearby; my green boba plushie on my desk.

My theory is right! Touching the hair is somehow letting me see through the eyes of my own body. I have no idea how, but it's for sure what's happening. Part of me wants to keep holding it—keep seeing the world as the real me for as long as I can. But another part of me is too disturbed by the fact that it isn't *me* who is actually inside my room. So, for now, I decide to stash it safely in a ring box atop the vanity in Jade's closet. I definitely don't want to lose it.

My phone chirps in my back pocket. A text from Ryan. I'm outside your house. Can you come to the front door real quick?

When I get there, I see him through the glass panel, sheepishly holding up an assortment of candy. I open the door with a questioning smile. "Jade and I had this thing," he says. "Whenever one of us was upset, the other would bring them their favorite candy as a pick-me-up. You've had a pretty terrible day. A pretty shit few days. So—I don't know what Megan's favorite candy is, which is why I look like I robbed a kid's Halloween bucket." He's got plain gummy worms and sour gummy bears in one hand and bars of Twix, Snickers, and KitKats in the other. He laughs nervously.

"Take your pick. Or all of 'em. Maybe they'll make you feel a little bit better?"

"Oh. Wow. Thanks." I'm gobsmacked—and a little mushy inside from the gesture. "It's Snickers, by the way. If you care to know." I reach out and take the candy bar from him.

"I'll remember that," Ryan says. "And I do."

"Oh . . . ummm . . . that's sweet," I say, musing about how I've never gotten a gift from a boy—unless you count Isaac in third grade who gave me a frog on the playground for Valentine's Day because Tiana was my favorite princess.

I know it's not entirely *me* getting this gift, and the circumstances of why he's being so sweet are bizarre. But since he actually knows I'm not Jade now, I think this does count in the gift-getting department. Right?

As I think on it, I don't immediately move to close the door, and Ryan doesn't immediately turn toward his Jeep. We simply stand there, eyes locked. I take an involuntary step forward, and he moves closer to me as well. I have a delirious moment where I envision us leaning into each other and kissing. And for all the world, if this was normal life, I think we would kiss. But this isn't normal life. Nothing about what we're tangled in is anywhere near the orbit of ordinary. Besides, he's likely only showing up and being so supportive because, in the end, it's Jade he wants to help.

"Thanks again," I say, stepping back. Although, all I want is to experience that kiss—even though he'd be kissing Jade, not me, not really.

"Bye, Megan. See you tomorrow," Ryan says softly, and I close the door before I reconsider this moment and dive into doing something idiotic.

Sixteen

The next day, I sit in a coffee shop that's located a block away from Fairburn's precinct, watching the door for Ryan, who should arrive at any moment after driving over from school.

When he walks inside, I can't help picturing his smile as he stood at Jade's front door yesterday, holding that load of candy. I bite the inside of my cheek, clear my head of the memory that threatens to make me grin big and goofy.

"Hey," I tell him when he reaches my table. My voice comes out breathier than I intend.

"Hey," he says back, sliding into the booth across from me. I swear there's an off-kilter note in his voice, too. But maybe I'm imagining it? Because *my* altered voice has everything to do with the fact that I can't get the image of a possible almost-kiss with him out of my head. Kept thinking about it all night, have been thinking about it way too much while waiting for him this afternoon. Ryan can't be plagued by the same feelings; I look like Jade, who is his platonic friend *only*.

And yet . . . maybe I'm not tripping, because he and I keep sitting there silent, and the same weirdness that spang up between us last night seems to be with us now.

I manage to force myself to shake it off and concentrate on what really matters.

"So, I've been thinking that you should speak to the detective by yourself," I suggest to Ryan. He looks puzzled. "I'm assuming most folks around know Jade's history with Lainey, since Fairburn is small, right?" I explain. "If I walk into the station with you when you ask about Lainey, your coach's wife might be less willing to give up info. Or me being there might get back to my parents, which won't go over well either."

"Yeah," he says. "You might have a point."

"Okay. So if you're cool going alone, I'll stay here."

"Good looking out," Ryan says, a slightly reedy quality still in his voice. "Glad you thought of that. It's really smart."

I don't know why I grin so wide in response; I just do.

As he strides away, I watch him through the coffee shop's large windows. He walks down an Old Town Fairburn street lined with wooden buildings that look like I've traveled a hundred years into the past. He disappears around the block that the police station is on, and after he hasn't reappeared for a good fifteen minutes, I start to let myself believe the extended time means he's getting information. If the detective immediately shot his request down, he would've come back already.

When he approaches the coffee shop another ten minutes later, I leap out of the booth and run to meet him on the sidewalk.

I take in his expression, which is a mixture of optimism and disappointment. "What happened?" I ask, my own spirits falling.

"I couldn't get an actual location," he tells me. "It is confidential. But I did find out Lainey didn't go to jail after she got arrested. She was sent to a group home. I convinced Mrs. Harris to let me write a letter that she'll forward to Lainey for me. It doesn't give anything away," he adds quickly. "Just asks how she's doing and if I can come see her. I'm positive that if she really is Jade, she'll be relieved I reached out and say yes."

"That was a good idea," I say, trying not to be too deflated. It's something, at least. "Let's think positive that 'Lainey' responds. But if she doesn't, we can start looking up nearby group homes." I stare into space for a second, a plan forming in my mind. "I can call them and say I'm one of Lainey's cousins who'd like to send her a care package. If they have a girl there by that name, they might at least give me an address—or off-site PO Box—to mail it to." I immediately take out my phone and google: *Group Homes for Minors in Georgia*.

"Share your search results with me; I'll start in on the list too," Ryan says as I'm bookmarking the results.

He and I sit on a nearby bench and start making calls. We get through four apiece, and none will give us any information on Lainey. They're unwilling to even say that she isn't a resident.

"This isn't gonna work," I say after I get off my latest call. I don't have the energy to keep up my former enthusiasm.

"Yeah," he says. "Probably not."

I check the time and reluctantly say, "Jade's parents are getting home soon. They want to have 'family time' before dinner." I roll my eyes.

"How are you even pulling this off with them?" he asks as we stand and start walking to his car. "How do you know what to say when they ask questions and shit?"

I shrug. "Honestly? I think they're so nervous about losing Jade again that they're scared to ask much of anything." I pause. "Also, what's more likely to occur to them: that their daughter is acting a little strange or her body has been jacked?"

He laughs. "You've got a point."

Ryan drops me off at the McCalls, and the next days are excruciating while we wait to see if Lainey will respond to the letter. I start to wonder if we'd be better off driving to the homes and lying that we're family members who've arrived for visiting hours. But then I realize what an impractical idea that is, and I'm back to wracking my brain for the next logical thing. I talk to Ava, who tries to help me brainstorm too, but her, Ryan, and I all remain stumped.

Finally, Ryan calls one night while I'm eating dinner with the McCalls. I silence the ring, even though my thumb itches to swipe right, and sit the phone beside my plate. Mom and Dad would tear into me for answering during family dinner. From everything I've gathered about Jade's parents, they wouldn't be pleased either.

A text from Ryan pops up on the screen. I got a letter from her.

I nearly choke on the forkful of roasted potatoes I've just swallowed. I slide the phone off the table and into my pocket before Mr. or Mrs. McCall can see the message.

"May I be excused?" I ask. "It's Ryan. I really want to talk to him."

Mr. and Mrs. McCall exchange one of their wordless conversations. Then, Mr. McCall waves me off and says, "Sure."

I call Ryan back as soon as I get to Jade's room. "What did the letter say?" I ask excitedly.

"She's at a group home only a few hours away!" he exclaims. "She says I can come if I don't mention the visit to anybody. You can get answers. *We* can get answers! She *must* be Jade if she wants to see me. I know it's a long shot, but maybe she'll know how to reverse the swaps. If so, we can break her out and go straight to Lainey. Give you and Jade your lives back!"

I can't speak at first. My throat is clogged as relieved tears stream down my face. I pray that Jade isn't as clueless as me. *God, please let her have realized that LC is behind it all.*

AS SHE HOLDS the poppy scarf that she stole from Tess before escaping, LC glimpses the dim interior of Tess's Volvo. The car is parked on a dark street lined with familiar glitzy mansions. LC sucks in a breath, her RSP—her residual sensory perception—confirming what she already suspected: Tess is staking out Jade's home. *Fuck.*

The closer Tess is to Megan, the closer she is to finding LC. And who knows what lies she'll tell Megan, and threats she might level, to make her cooperate! Tess is a master manipulator.

Megan's parents pull into the driveway, drawing LC's attention. She drops Tess's scarf into her lap as Malinda and Lincoln Allen chirp hellos. "We got you your favorites: lo mein and a mountain of fortune cookies!" says Mr. Allen, kissing LC's temple. She longs for this doting gesture from her true parent. Maybe something like it did happen once—if she could only remember. "Are you okay, Meggie?" he asks, clearly responding to the sudden sadness on his daughter's face.

"I am," LC says, putting on a convincing smile. She nods toward the takeout. "Just starved."

Mr. Allen helps her off the swing, tucking her into his side with a hug. "Let's go dig in, then! I'm starving too, and your mother was a tyrant who wouldn't let me open a container on the drive home. I think she delights in your dear dad's pain and suffering," says Mr. Allen with exaggerated gravity.

"Because tonight is family dinner night," Mrs. Allen laughs, elbowing her husband in the ribs.

Lincoln chuckles alongside her, and their joy blankets LC, soothing the rawest of her fears and nerves, as she walks into the Allen home. She muses, not for the first time, that it's funny . . . something about being here with them, in this house, makes her feel more like herself, even though she's pretending to be Megan. It's terrible and a further assault on Megan. But somehow LC feels like her childhood is returning to her the more she settles into life with the Allens.

She wonders if it's the feeling of being loved that's having this effect. Maybe it's triggering a deeply buried emotional memory that Tess couldn't steal. LC likes the thought that some part of her childhood self refused to be erased.

She has seen herself as being trapped, in a way, by not knowing her past. Trapped without a sense of identity. But maybe what she needs is to see it as being free. Free to define herself through her actions. So, the question is, who does she want to be? And what does she have to do now to be that person?

Because with Tess closing in, decisions have to be made.

Seventeen

Brighthaven Youth Home allows visitors on Saturday mornings. I wait in the well-kept lobby of the single-story building with light blue walls and harsh overhead lighting. Beside me on the plasticky beige couch, Ava holds my hand. My ex-friend would've been well within her rights to tell me to kick rocks when I asked her to come for moral support, but staying entangled with this mystery is letting her be a real-life Nancy Drew, and she wouldn't pass that up for anything. Also, she's just that good a person.

I anxiously peer around the lobby desk at the door to the visitor's room, waiting for it to open again. The frosted glass makes it impossible to see anything that's happening inside. Ryan went in about ten minutes ago to meet "Lainey Carter" first, to have a moment alone with the girl we're near-positive is his missing friend.

"I'm really glad you came," I tell Ava, squeezing her hand. Her presence helps the wait pass more easily. It also makes it clearer to me that Ava's qualities—caring, trustworthy, dependable—are what I should've been looking for and valuing in a friend all along.

"I want you to know something," I say to her. "Back—you know, when we were close—I was low-key jealous of how easily you embrace who you are without stressing what other people think. I wish that was that easy for me." The confession doesn't make my mistakes any better, but I at least owe her the full truth.

Ava gapes at me, red splotches splattering her face. "I—I didn't know you felt that way."

"I do," I say. "If I ever get my body back, I wanna try just being . . . Megan, whatever that means. I think that's something I need to figure out." I pause, staring down at my lap. "It's always been hard to see where I fit. Sometimes, I feel like I don't fit perfectly anywhere. I don't know . . . does that sound crazy?"

Ava slings an arm around my shoulders. "One: It's not an *if* you get your body back. We *will* get it back. Two: It sounds within the range of the normal shit we all go through. And for what it's worth, I regret stuff I did in our friendship too."

"You do?"

She nods. "I was super clingy and selfish. It was cruddy of me to try to force you to *only* hang out with me. I like having one hard-core bestie, but it should've been okay with me for you to have other close friends. I think I was jealous. And scared you'd replace me. Which . . . I guess I helped make it happen anyway."

Before I can respond, my phone vibrates in my lap.

A text from Ryan: Come back and meet Jade.

"It's her!" Ava squeals, hugging me tight.

"Sounds like it," I say excitedly as another text comes through.

Staff is in here, so be careful what you say

167

I stand, suddenly flooded with nerves.

When Ava and I step into the visitor's room, I see a girl with medium-brown skin, hazel eyes, and straight, chin-length auburn hair seated beside Ryan. (How weird to think that's *LC*'s real face.) She stares back at me, eyes wide with shock. And I get it. *God, I get it.* Even though Ryan would've explained the situation, there's no preparing for the horror of seeing your own body being piloted by someone else.

From Jade's perspective, I'm a thief. Everything I'm wearing down to my jeans and yellow sweater and mini purse strapped across my chest—even my face—is *hers*. I'm not the one who robbed Jade of her life, but it doesn't change that I'm still the one walking around inside it while she's trapped in here.

"I'm so sorry," I blurt as Ava and I sit across from Jade and Ryan. There's one staff member in the room, standing in the far corner, currently looking at his phone.

"I can't believe she jumped again. That she just . . . ditched my body," Jade says, her voice low. "Are my parents okay?"

I nod. "Totally fine. They were worried like crazy when they thought you ran away, but now that they think you've come home, they're better." A startling familiarity washes over me as I gaze at Jade—or LC, I should say. Strangely, it's the exact inexplicable niggling you get when you meet a new person and swear they're somebody you know from somewhere. There's no way I'd know Lainey Carter's face—I'd never heard of her before seeing her name in Jade's case file at the McCalls. But . . . her eyes. The exact mix of brown and green in Lainey's eyes—some kind of recognition pricks at my memory.

Get it together, Megan. You're tripping.

"Are you all right?" I ask Jade, focusing on why we've come. "Is it . . . scary in here?"

Jade fidgets with her hands folded together on the table. "I'm fine," she says, but I don't miss how she glances over at the staff member.

"We're going to get you out of here," Ryan whispers, then says to me, "The swap happened the same way it did with you—the drug LC said was Molly, waking up in the different body . . . Except then Jade was arrested."

It's crazy that as bad as my experience was—getting locked out, carted off to the hospital, and sent home with the McCalls—it could've been worse.

"Arrested for what?" I ask her.

Jade's eyes dart to the staff member again, and then to a camera in a corner of the room.

Ryan scoots closer to her.

"LC had outstanding warrants," she says, her voice so quiet, I have to strain to hear. "For stealing. What I've gathered is that her parents died when she was younger, she has a pattern of running from foster homes, and she's had a lot of run-ins with the police for stealing." As Jade tells me this, I can't help feeling a moment of sadness for LC. Or, at least, for the girl she once was.

"How long are you supposed to be in here?" I ask. "Not that we'll let—"

The door opens and another staff member comes in and starts talking to the one in the corner. They immediately become animated. Entirely focused on their discussion.

"Look," Jade says, leaning closer to us, her tone urgent. "I can't say much, but you have to know a couple things. We're mixed up in some really dangerous shit, but someone is helping us. I've been meeting . . ." She glances back at the staff, who continue to talk, and then back at us. "I've been meeting with an FBI agent."

"You've been doing *what*?!" I say. Ava and I both lean in closer to her.

"Lainey's involved with criminals," Jade explains quickly. "They've been looking for her, and those same folks might go after people with ties to her. I can't say anything else. The FBI agent warned me it's too dangerous to talk to anybody about it. But when I see her again, I can have her call you, Megan."

"Can *I* call *her*?!" I ask. If there's somebody out there who's helping, I don't want to wait!

Jade shakes her head. "I don't even have her number. She just showed up one day; shocked the shit out of me when she told me she knew I wasn't the real Lainey Carter. But she visits frequently and promises that if I do what she says, she'll get me out of here and back to my life. And rule number one is that I can't talk about it, so you guys really need to go. Like I said, this is all really dangerous."

"Is LC herself dangerous?" I ask.

"Extremely."

"Our nape piercings, that's how the swapping is done, right?"

Jade bites her lip. "Please stop asking questions. I promise, I'll have her call you when she comes here again; she'll give you all the answers."

"I'm sure she would understand if you talk to me!" I say, frustrated. "I'm in this mess, too!"

"Look," Jade whispers. "All I want is my life back. And I'm not going to do anything to jeopardize that, okay? I shouldn't have even answered the letter. She told me not to contact anyone. But I'm just . . . I'm so lonely. And scared." The emotions are plain on her face.

She pushes back from the table and stands. "I'm gonna go, so y'all can do the same."

"Hold up!" Ryan says. "Stay. Please."

Jade shakes her head. "I— Sorry. I can't." She leans forward and wraps Ryan in a fierce hug. "I miss you," she whispers.

One of the staff members coughs loudly. "Finish up the visit, Carter," he says. "Time to go."

When we get back to Jade's house, Ryan and I explore an idea I had on the drive home. There's no way I'm waiting for a call from that agent to get answers. And I've come across enough TikTok jokes and #HorrorTok vids that mention the dark web to know it contains forums about some seriously shady stuff. We know the FBI is involved, and there's a criminal element, so maybe something about it has leaked onto dark-web forums? Ryan is uneasy about getting on the actual dark web, though, so I suggest we search TikTok's dark-web corner. While Ryan scrolls through posts on his phone, I do the same on mine, both of us sitting on Jade's bed, the remaining candy from his gas-station raid between us. After a whole lotta nothing, I come across a conspiracy account with few followers that swears the government is developing and testing technology that can place a person's mind in a different body.

"Look!" I wave my phone at Ryan.

He scoots closer to me, and we view the video together. The guy goes on a full rant about how there are people walking around with their brains jacked—the government's lab rats. He says different governments around the world have invested in the tech, envisioning a future where dictators can live forever, hopping from one body to the next, and where they can charge rich people a fortune to do the same. The guy thinks we're all in danger of a time when our bodies can be stolen, just like that.

I blink, my skin crawling at the thought that *I* could be a lab rat. Is that why LC did this to me? If the government is conducting research, a criminal cell who wants to sell the tech on the black market might be doing the same—you know, coming up with their own version? Is LC working with them or something? I fidget with the phone, trying not to become too rattled by the thought. "You all right?" Ryan asks with clear concern.

I give a shaky laugh. Wave my phone. "Hell no. How can I not be extremely disturbed after hearing about what this guy says is going down, if I've actually experienced it?"

Ryan reaches over and grabs my hand. "I'd be creeped out too."

The warmth of his hand against mine helps center me. And this time, I don't push the *zing* away. I clutch his hand back. Breathe in. Breathe out.

"Thanks," I say quietly.

He gives me this small, almost-shy smile. "Anytime." I think he feels the *zing* too, because he clears his throat. Releases my hand. "This might just be a crackpot's page, and I hope that isn't what's going down, but do you think we should try to see if this person really knows something?"

"I think we should follow any lead we come across," I answer, sure about that fact. Which is why I then create a throwaway account and post a comment.

NoNameGirl333: Interesting! How would people's minds get swapped if this is happening?

A few minutes crawl by without a response. I keep the video up, refreshing the comments, even though, logically, I know I won't get an answer straightaway.

"Let's keep looking for additional mentions," I suggest to Ryan so I don't lose my mind while waiting.

Concentrating on the search helps, but we don't come across another post on body swapping. "Maybe we've just gotta brave the dark web," I say.

It takes Ryan a minute to agree. "Okay," he agrees eventually. He sounds nervous as hell, though. Honestly, I'm freaking too.

A google search gives us the basics for how to do it, and the anonymizing browser is halfway downloaded to my laptop when *I* get cold feet. I can't explain why—it's just a gut feeling that something bad is going to happen. Like we're inviting more trouble. "Actually, let's wait a little longer to see if the TikToker responds," I say, quickly canceling the download.

"Fine by me," Ryan replies, sounding hella relieved.

I flop back on the bed to just wait. *Why does* everything *have to be so hard?!*

I don't realize I said it out loud until Ryan responds, "For real, though. This is . . . I don't even know if there's a strong enough word. All I know is that I'm scared as hell, all the time, for Jade and for you, and this is all just so fucking messed-up. I feel like we've all gotten trapped in the latest Jordan Peele movie or something." He laughs shakily. "But this is y'all's real lives that are in danger."

I sit back up. Reach for Ryan and hug him. I've been thinking all about me, but he's clearly going through a lot with all this too. "It must've been really hard for you, seeing Jade like that?"

"It messed me up. A lot." He hugs me back. We stay like that for a few seconds until my phone vibrates against my leg. I pick it up and see a notification that the TikTok poster has responded.

Thank God.

I open the app.

ChadSpillzTea: They do it with nanotechnology. They download people's consciousness onto a microchip and implant it into a different body.

Nanotech. I reach back and finger my piercing—a small metal object inserted into my flesh. Something that could contain a microchip. "I knew the piercings had something to do with it!" I shout, squeezing Ryan again. "I *know* I'm onto something!" I tell him, then stiffen when I realize that I basically just jumped him—and this time I don't have a good excuse. "Sorry," I sputter.

"It's cool," he says, holding me tight. "But what do we do with it? How can we use it to help you and Jade?"

"Yeah. So. Ummm . . ." The way his arms remain locked around me makes it hard to think straight. Reluctantly, I pull away and gather myself. "Can you look at this thing up close?" I ask. I shift forward and lift up my hair, exposing my barbell. "I'm just curious—do you see anything that's weird? Like . . . I don't know . . . markings? A tiny slit for data transfer? *Alien hieroglyphics?*" Okay, I'm not serious about that last part. . . . Although I *have* been in the realm of the outlandish since waking up at Nathan's.

Ryan softly touches my neck and leans close enough that I can feel his warm breath on my skin. "Hard to say much of anything about it," he says. "I mean, it does seem like it's maybe a bit bigger than a regular piercing—the part that goes into your skin, that is." He leans even closer. "And there's, like, a teeny sort of opening? Really, really small. Where something could be inserted, maybe?" He sits back. "I don't want to mess with it, though. What if I break it or hurt you some kind of way?"

"Yeah," I say, letting my hair fall. "That probably isn't a good idea."

We sit quiet for a moment.

"How about this?" I say, after giving it some thought. "I text LC that I know about the nanotech and microchips. I can claim it's because I was approached by one of the criminals she's tangled up with. I can lie and say they told me everything because they're looking for her and promised not to hurt me if I tell them her location. I can promise LC that I'll give them a false one if she does what I want." As I say the words, it sounds crazy, but also like maybe it's a legit plan.

"You really came up with all that on the fly?" Ryan asks.

I fight a smile at the amazement in his voice.

"It's pretty good, isn't it?" I reply, impressed with myself too. "I'll text LC right now." I keep my eyes pinned to my screen; it's best not to let them stray to Ryan because those two hugs and his soft hand and warm breath on my neck have got me off-kilter.

I've just finished writing her when Ryan's phone dings. "It's my parents. I've gotta go," he says. Then that slightly shy smile crosses his face again. He stands, shoving his phone in his pocket. "I'll call you later. We can plan things out more."

"Sounds good," I say, majorly disappointed that he's leaving. "I'll let you know the moment LC responds."

When LC hasn't messaged back late into the evening, I'm exhausted from the eventful day but can't sleep. I keep staring at my screen and waiting—wondering what's going on with her. Is she angry and figuring out how to handle me? Or is she going to ignore me completely? Finally, the phone vibrates, and it's a call from an unknown number. I hit the answer button, anxious.

Silence greets my hello.

"LC?" I say.

"This is Agent Meadows," comes a woman's voice. "I'm from the FBI. Jade McCall gave me your number."

Eighteen

I sit in a booth near the back of an Old Town diner and watch a white woman, who appears to be in her late twenties, maybe early thirties, stride toward me. I assume she's Agent Meadows, who maddeningly wouldn't say much when she called, only that it was safest to talk in person. Her snug cream pants and expensive-looking green blazer don't hide the bulge near her waist. My mouth goes dry when I glimpse her gun. It makes sense that she has one, of course. And I know she isn't here to hurt me. But still . . . it's difficult to push the unease away. Meadows *is* a white cop carrying a gun, and I'm a Black kid.

"Hi!" I'm mostly calm as Agent Meadows slides into the booth opposite me.

"Hello!" she says warmly, extending her hand. "Despite the circumstances, I'm glad to meet you, Megan."

"Me too," I say.

"You've become mixed up in some upsetting stuff. I can't imagine how disorienting this has been for you."

I nod, a sudden lump forming in my throat. Finally, some-one with the power to help knows what happened. And she *believes* me!

"Don't worry," she says. "This case is my number one priority. I'm going to make sure you get your body back."

I let go of her hand, wanting to cry. "That's what I was hoping to hear. I just want my normal life."

Her smile is sympathetic. "I imagine that you do. And until then, I'm also going to make sure that you're safe."

"Good morning! What can I get you two?" The elderly Black woman standing beside our booth wears a sunny smile. It wavers when she looks to Agent Meadows, wariness shadowing her face. "How are you doing today, sweetie?" she says directly to me, and I don't miss the unspoken *Are you all right? Is this woman bothering you?*

"I'm fine," I assure her.

"If that's the case, what will you have? I'm Ms. Grace, by the way. You won't find a finer latte, cherry cobbler, or hash brown scramble in the whole of the southeast," she says, winking at me.

I feel lighter and more relaxed in her presence; it's a solace only a Black grandmotherly woman could bestow. "Those all sound yummy, but I'm vegan," I say apologetically.

She stabs a finger at one of the menus on the table. *Auntie Grace's* is printed across the top in cursive gold letters. "I've got vegan peach pie and vegan tea cakes."

I hadn't planned on eating, but I skipped breakfast—too anx-ious—and my stomach rumbles. It must be loud as heck, because

Ms. Grace raises an eyebrow, poises her pen over her notepad, and waits. Her body language says *you ain't gonna tell me no*. Between Mom, both my grandmas, and a slew of older Black aunts and women cousins, I know better than to argue. I am not about to have the smackdown laid on me by Ms. Grace.

"I'll have the vegan tea cakes and iced tea."

She smiles approvingly. "Coming right up for you, baby." She turns to Agent Meadows; her demeanor grows coarser. "And you, ma'am?" Her eyes flick to the gun, as mine did.

"I'll have a coffee, one sugar, and a splash of cream, please. I'll also take a slice of the cherry cobbler you recommended," Agent Meadows says. "Thank you so much, ma'am."

As soon as Ms. Grace disappears into the kitchen, Agent Meadows leans forward, dropping her voice low. "I'm not sure how much you know, but just so you understand the gravity, this stuff you're involved in is a dangerous situation. I'm going to have to ask for your complete trust, cooperation, and discretion. For your own safety."

Any measure of comfort I felt vanishes. "I'll do anything I can."

"Good," she says, nodding. We're both silent for a minute as Ms. Grace brings out our drinks and food. "Thank you, ma'am," Agent Meadows says.

"Let me know if you need anything else," Ms. Grace says, looking at me before leaving us alone.

I sip my iced tea and wait for Agent Meadows to continue. "When was the last time you saw Lainey?" she finally asks. "Have you seen her since the swap?"

"Um . . . a couple of times," I say.

"Where?"

Before I give her any information, it occurs to me that I should have probably started this meeting by being a little more careful.

"Can I see a badge?" I ask. Maybe her talk of the danger I'm in has me rattled, but it's best to double-check.

Agent Meadows smiles, reaching inside her blazer. "Smart girl."

She flashes me FBI credentials that have her full name (Tess Meadows), badge number, and photo. "May I see your phone?" she asks as she's sliding the leather wallet back into her blazer's pocket.

"Yeah. Sure. There's messages from Lainey on it." I hand it over, but she doesn't look at the messages. She switches the phone off and sets it beside her on the table.

"Another safety precaution," says Meadows. "You never know what information your cell is picking up and who's accessing it."

"That's creepy," I say, reaching for the phone.

She lays a hand atop it. "Let me hold on to this until you leave. Is that all right?"

"Um, sure." Although . . . I'm perfectly capable of keeping my phone off and in my own possession. Something about her refusal to give it back just doesn't sit right.

It's no big deal. She's on your side, I remind myself.

"Look," she says, maybe sensing my hesitance, "we're just establishing our trust here, right? You don't know me, and I don't know you. In fact, all I know about you is that you're mixed up in something dangerous and illegal. I'm willing to take you at your word that it wasn't by choice, but I've been lied to before—"

"I'm not lying," I say quickly. "Not about anything."

"Good," she says. "So, Lainey: When and where did you last see her?"

Graysonville. Where I live. Something stops me from sharing it immediately, though. If I admit it's where I'm from, then Meadows will go there looking for LC—and LC is living in my house, with my family. What I want—*all* I want—is for Meadows to arrest LC and force her to swap back. But if LC is involved with dangerous criminals, this could bring my family to their attention. "If you go after Lainey, and there's shady people also after her, are the people around her in any kind of danger?" I ask.

"Is she living with your family?" Meadows says. "The FBI can put measures in place to keep them safe. We're doing the exact thing for Jade's parents."

"Jade's parents know about this?" I say, shocked.

"No, no," she says. "They have no idea."

So they're being surveilled without knowing it? That's disturbing. Also, even though I want to believe her that they're safe, how many stories do you hear about cops fumbling—or simply just not caring enough—with certain people? "What kind of criminals is Lainey involved with?" I ask. "Rogue government scientists? Bioterrorists? The organized mob?" None of my guesses sound impossible after hearing that guy's TikTok rant about who's developing this tech.

Agent Meadows frowns. "I can't tell you anything specific. It's classified, and the less you know, the safer you are. All you need to know is that the swaps are done with illegal technology developed by these criminals. Everything about the process is unregulated and unsafe. Swapping itself can have potentially nasty side effects."

"Nasty side effects like being *trapped* in a different body after a certain amount of time?" *Please, no.*

"Sorry. That's classified too." Meadows, of course, replies with one of her maddening nonanswers. "How about we just focus on getting your body back? I know me not being able to tell you much else is frustrating and scary, but, again, it's for your saf—"

"I've already gotten hurt!" I snap, frustrated. "And it appears that I'm not safe at all—likely *can't* be made safe whatsoever by anybody! Me simply knowing body swapping is real puts me permanently at risk, even if you find Lainey, yes? So, please, tell me at least *some* of what I'm asking."

"Things can get much, much worse, Megan," Meadows says, but I don't back down.

"The piercings?" I press. "Is that how the swaps are done? The barbell is the upload/download port, and it houses microchips that our consciousness gets downloaded to, right?"

Surprise flickers across Agent Meadows's face, followed by a momentary scowl. "Where did you hear that?" she asks lightly.

"I guessed about the port and then saw something on TikTok that mentioned body swapping. When I asked about how it could be done in the comments, the creator said nanotech and microchips are used. He said swapping is the government's creation, *not* something developed by criminals," I add. "Is there truth to that?

Did this start with the government and criminals stole it?"

Agent Meadows sighs. "You left a public comment on the *internet*? That's . . . not good, Megan. The cell of criminals involved with the tech troll for people who know about it, to keep everything underground. That person on TikTok is likely a part of the cell. That's why he linked it to the government and didn't mention its illegal origins."

Shit. Oh My God. Shit. A lump forms in my throat.

"I barely said anything," I clarify. "Just asked a question."

"Doesn't matter. They just wanted your ISP address, Megan. Your location." She pauses. "They know where you are now, and they know you're aware of their activity. I can still make this all right for you, though. Protect you from them. But it's become more imperative that I arrest Lainey quickly." Agent Meadows pulls a pen and business card out of a pocket. She flips the card over to the back and pushes it and the pen toward me. "If you know where Lainey is staying, write down the address."

My hands are clammy. It's best to do as she asks. Logically, I get that. But . . . I can't shake off the bad feeling about giving Meadows my family's address. I really want to keep them out of this as much as possible. Meadows has made it plenty clear how dangerous the whole situation is. "Lainey was staying at my house after she stole my body and started posing as me," I say. "But she's staying with a friend this week while my parents are out of town. I'm not sure who."

Agent Meadows casts me a doubtful look. "You don't have relatives? There's no grandparents, cousins, or family friends who you'd usually stay with?"

"No," I lie. "All of our family lives out of town, and my parents are super strict about not missing school. Oh! Wait!" I exclaim. "I can give you my school address."

"I'll take that, sure. But if I apprehend Lainey at your school, I'll be formally arresting *you*. Do you really want that on *your* record? Or for your parents to endure such an ordeal and your reputation to be ruined?"

I wince.

"I didn't think so," Meadows says. "There's a way that you can locate Lainey, wherever she's staying. I can get to her outside of school. You can track her for me by tuning in to something called RSP—residual sensory perception. On our call, you said you had an object that belonged to your original self. Did you bring it as I asked?"

"Yes," I say, confused. I have no idea what residual sensory perception is and am still wobbly from her mentioning *Megan* getting an arrest record. My showcase would be off the table, no college would accept me, and my future would be trashed. Obviously, the most important thing is getting my body back, but I want my *life* back, too.

"RSP is a side effect of body swapping," Meadows continues.

I force myself to set aside my worry about the arrest and listen, since she seems to finally be giving me some answers.

"Once you've been in a body, holding something that has touched it—like clothes, a hairpin, or even jewelry—lets you see through the body's eyes in short flashes. It works with anything that has traces of the body's DNA."

That's precisely what happened to me both times I held on to the violet hair and when I shoved LC!

"If you use the object you brought to tap into the RSP and tell me where Lainey is, I'll leave this diner and head to her immediately," finishes Meadows.

"I have it. . . . ," I tell her, scrambling for a new idea that gets around taking her to my house. "But I have to go to the bathroom first. Is that okay? I'll be right back."

Agent Meadows's expression sours. It's only a brief thing. Probably just annoyance. But something about it spurs a new wave of hesitation. Can I *really* trust her? Yes, she showed me credentials. But those can be faked. How many cop dramas have I watched with Dad where that's happened?

When she tells me she doesn't mind if I use the restroom, her demeanor is warm again. Once I'm inside the stall with the door locked, I press my back against it and just breathe, not knowing what the hell to do. Do I trust Meadows? And what are my choices if I don't?

I jump at the sound of the restroom door swinging open. Footsteps click against the tile and then there's a knock on my stall. "Are you okay, honey?" A breath whooshes out of me when the voice belongs to the diner's owner. I thank the universe for the lifeline.

I exit the stall, tell Ms. Grace I'm fine, and ask if I can borrow her phone.

"Is this about that white lady out there?" she asks, fishing it out of her apron's pocket.

"Sort of?"

She gives me a pitying look. "Whatever you need, if I can help, I will."

"Thank you," I respond, grateful. "I only need to use your internet. I just want to make sure the woman is a cop like she says she is . . . to make sure I can trust her." I tell Ms. Grace the truth.

She sighs and hands over the phone. I google *Tess Meadows* and find a *Tallahassee Democrat* article about a Florida-born Detective Tess Meadows who is a hometown hero. Detective Meadows told the newspaper that she focuses her work in law enforcement around giving minors a second chance when the system otherwise wouldn't. There's no photo, and it doesn't verify Tess Meadows is an FBI agent, exactly. . . . I think about calling Ryan to get his opinion, but I don't know his number by heart. I try Ava instead; she doesn't answer. I reread the article, decide for myself that what it gives me is enough. Plus, I imagine I can't stay locked in the bathroom for much longer before Meadows comes to check on me.

When I approach the table, she's on the phone. She ends the call, clearly angry again. "Look," she says before I can sit down. "In addition to having called attention to yourself online, you're in possession of an illegal implant and have engaged in illegal activity. I was trying to help you out of a sketchy situation, but you're making my job—which is to protect the wider public, first and foremost—difficult. At this point, if you refuse to cooperate and tell me where Lainey could be staying, I can charge you with a felony and put you in a juvenile detention center."

My knees lock. "I—I don't understand. I didn't do anything wrong! *I'm* a victim!"

Meadows shakes her head. "By having illegal hardware embedded in you, you're basically a criminal yourself in the eyes of the law and my superiors. I can only protect you from a felony charge *and* outside threats if you cooperate with me in every way. Do you get that?"

I do. I really, really do. She's turned off Nice Cop mode. She's trying to intimidate me—and it's working. "Lainey is in Graysonville, Georgia," I sputter. "I'll drive there with you now and use RSP to pin down where she is," I offer. She's not getting my family's address, legit agent or not, but I don't want to go to jail, either. I've got to buy time to figure out how to get back on Meadows's good side *and* keep my family safe.

I better come up with something good. And make it believable this time.

Nineteen

Agent Meadows walks me to a black Volvo SUV. When she opens the passenger door and gestures for me to get in, I'm seized by a sudden panic. I'm about to get into a car and drive away from Fairburn with a cop who isn't too happy with me. That plus the warnings you get from the time you're little to not go anywhere with strangers make me want to rethink this whole plan.

But I force myself to climb into the vehicle, and as I do, I remind myself we're headed toward Graysonville, which is home. It marginally helps.

Meadows starts the engine and pulls out of the parking lot behind Auntie Grace's. We drive in tense silence for a bit.

Then, out of nowhere, Meadows says, "Sorry if I was tough with you back at the diner. This case is really, really important to me. Sometimes I have trouble keeping my emotions out of it." She sounds raw. Vulnerable.

"That's okay," I say, taken aback. I guess I'm glad she feels that strongly; it means she'll fight strongly to set things right.

I stare out the tinted window, realizing maybe I can take advantage of this new mood of hers.

"I know you can't tell me much about anything involving the nanotech," I say carefully, "but it'd be good to know more about Lainey's background. Just so I can understand why she did this to me."

"Sure," she says. "Lainey's had a difficult past. It's what made me feel for her when I first met her. What made me want to help her."

"Help her?" I say, confused. "I thought you were trying to arrest her."

Meadows glances over at me, a wry smile in place. "*Now* I am. It didn't start out that way." She looks toward the road again. "Lainey is exceptionally good at coaxing people to lower their guard and trust her. That girl is a master manipulator. I figured that out too late." She pauses. "Something you and I have in common, I guess."

I nod, biting my cheeks. "If you weren't trying to arrest her, how'd you two meet?"

"Lainey tried to lift my wallet while she was living on the streets. I confronted her, told her I was an agent. Instead of arresting her, I asked if I could buy her a meal and chat with her about her situation, see if there was anything I could do to help. It turned into me fostering Lainey. This is something I don't tell most people, but I used to have a younger sister who Lainey reminded me a lot of. My sister passed when she was sixteen years old and was a runaway too. I couldn't save her. I thought maybe Lainey could be my chance to make things right." Meadows stares straight ahead, eyes fixed on the highway we just got on. She seems legitimately upset. "I failed Lainey too; I was investigating the illegal tech, and that's how Lainey got involved with it. The people behind it found out about my investigation and went after Lainey instead of me directly. They convinced her to steal the hardware I'd managed to get my hands on to use as evidence. Lainey was supposed to hand it over to them. She ran, instead—from me *and* them."

"Why? Is she looking for a way to sell it?" I ask, finally piecing together LC's likely endgame. On the show *Immortal Futures*, tech that can make people live forever sells for a fortune. Maybe LC swapped with Jade and then me to stay ahead of Meadows and the criminals until she can sell it.

"I plan to ask her," Meadows says. "Seems a little unlikely she'd think she'd be able to find people to buy it without being caught."

I nod. "I'm sorry about your sister," I say.

"Me too," Meadows responds.

Afterward, a comfortable silence settles between us, the atmosphere in the car no longer as tense. I'm tackling how to use RSP to help Meadows arrest LC without giving up my home address when things happen in quick succession: Meadows takes a sip of her to-go coffee from Auntie Grace's, sees something in the rearview mirror, drops the cup to grab the wheel, jerks the car hard to the left. A car zooms by, way too close. Meadows curses and looks at her feet, where the coffee cup fell. Shakes her head. "At least it was almost empty."

As she bends down to grab the cup, her hair falls to the side. It takes barely a second before she settles back into her seat, but not before I glimpse something. Something at the nape of her neck.

Something metallic.

I startle. Why would an FBI agent have the piercing, too?

My heart races. I grip my seat belt. Suck in a breath as quietly as possible.

There could be a good explanation. Right? I saw her badge. And that article online. She's definitely FBI.

A cautioning, urgent voice inside whispers that legitimate cops can also be crooked. And now, I can't stop—or hide—my trembling.

"I'm guessing you saw my piercing a moment ago," Meadows says stiffly.

Yes! No! I won't tell anybody! I have no idea what to say, how she'll take it. So I say nothing.

I jolt when Meadows pats my hand that's still gripping the seat belt. "It's all right. I got it while undercover. Lainey's seen it too. It's part of why she ran. She's developed the delusion that I'm in league with the tech's developers. I need to keep the piercing confidential, of course—that's why I didn't tell you before."

I nod mutely, the tightness in my chest easing. Although something doesn't quite add up. "I thought you said that Lainey was sort of linked up with the tech people herself? Wouldn't she have known you weren't on their side?"

"Honestly?" Meadows says. "I think that Lainey's difficult past made it impossible for her to trust anyone. Even me."

Makes sense. "Did you . . . Have you experienced a swap?" I ask. If she's sharing more, I'm curious.

"Yes. Numerous times. I know, intimately, the hell you've

gone through. I let myself be used for swapping experiments. It's very unsettling, to say the least. And it's an incredible violation that it was done to you forcibly."

I clasp my hands in my lap, unable to form a response. The anger and the *ache* to have my life back steal my voice.

"Hey," Meadows says gently. "We're on our way to fix this for you. Can you try tuning into RSP now? I'd like to get Lainey's current location, and then have you keep track of her as we near Graysonville. I've gotten close to Lainey before, and she's managed to evade me."

"Okay," I say. I still don't know what to do if Lainey is at my house. I guess I'll just have to trust Meadows?

I slide the ring box out of my pocket, open it, and hold the violet hair. I clench my teeth when the vertigo sweeps through me, pay attention to the flash of images. LC's surroundings are unfamiliar; she's at a food truck park somewhere—not my home. *Thank God.* "Can I use my phone?" I ask Agent Meadows, blinking to clear the haze that lingers after I place the hair back into the box. "I don't recognize where Lainey is and need to check a street sign."

Agent Meadows nods to my phone resting in the center console. When I switch it on, there are a bunch of texts from my real number. I angle the phone away from Meadows and go to my messages, biting down hard on the inside of my lip as I read what LC sent.

I know you're in a car with Tess Meadows

She's the danger I warned you about! Everything she's probably told you is a lie

Make up an excuse to turn around and go back to Jade's house. Don't tell Tess about this text

Do what I say or I swear I will ruin your life. For good

And not only your life, your family's life too. I don't want to, Megan, but I will

I grip the phone, not understanding. How the hell does LC know I'm with Meadows and driving to Graysonville? But then, I get it. *She must have something of Jade's and is using RSP, too! She's keeping tabs on me!* LC swapped bodies with Jade before she swapped with me, so she has the ability to use RSP and track the body I'm in. My pulse races. But not because I've realized she can keep tabs on me—because of her threat. LC has way too much control over my life and my future. She could do *anything*, and I would be blamed for it. She could murder someone!

I have to get Meadows to turn the car around without making her suspicious or pissed off.

Miraculously, a good idea occurs to me despite my panic.

"Shoot. Lainey isn't in Graysonville anymore," I say. "She's on a bus that's either traveling through Macon or Charleston, according to the street sign I read. She's left town." The desperation in my voice *is* one-hundred-percent real. *Please buy this.*

"Are you sure?" Meadows asks. "You could see that clearly?"

"I'm sure," I say.

Meadows slams a hand against the steering wheel. "Shit!" It takes her a minute to gather her composure. She exits the highway and takes a turn that places us on I-75 headed south instead of north.

The drive back to Fairburn is completely silent. I itch to check my phone for more messages from LC. But I figure it's better not to draw Meadows's attention to it. I don't want her to take it again.

When we reach the outskirts of Fairburn, she says, "Why don't you come back to my office? You can keep checking in to see if LC's back in Graysonville."

"Um, actually, Jade's parents are expecting me home," I lie. "They keep really strict tabs on me. And I'm sure they'll freak out and think I've run away if I don't go back." They actually think I'm with Ryan and are fine with it. But Meadows buys the lie— luckily, since LC specifically told me to go back to Jade's house, and she'll be able to see if I don't.

"I'll call you soon," Meadows says when she drops me a block away from the McCalls'. "Keep using RSP to track Lainey, and I'll be in touch for regular updates."

I climb out the SUV and text Ryan, trembling, as soon as Meadows drives off.

Can you come over? Right now?

I need major help.

AN ACUTE PRESSURE eases from LC's chest when she catches flashes of Megan walking into Jade's house.

Phew.

But LC doesn't cheer in victory. Only relief—one she knows is temporary. There's still a battle ahead.

LC sets aside the object she uses to track Jade's body—one of Jade's hair bands—feeling bad for bluffing to Megan that she'd hurt her family. *It was the only choice,* she reminds herself, *as always*. She is tired of telling herself that. So damn tired. She wants it all to end. It's time for her to make it end. It's time to switch her methods up in ways Tess would never think she had the strength or the smarts to do. Time to be the person LC has decided she wants to be.

LC googles an address in Jacksonville, Florida, with tingling fingers. She looks at satellite images of a building she never wanted to see again. Never wants to step foot inside again. Her heart pounds, thinking about what she's going to attempt. And she wonders if the decisions that she's making about what to sacrifice, what to fight for, and where to draw a line are the right ones.

Twenty

My brain is spinning as I start up the stairs to Jade's bedroom. I don't even know which of the things that just happened I should be most worried about: Lying to the FBI? LC's threat? The shady folks tracking my ISP address? Agent Meadows's piercing?

"Jade?" The voice makes me inhale sharply.

I turn to see Mr. McCall standing behind me.

"You startled me," I say, pressing a hand on my chest. "I thought you weren't home yet."

"We're not *supposed* to be home," Jade's dad says. "Why don't you come into the living room and talk to us for a minute?"

No. I can't deal with these people right now. "Um, I'm actually pretty tired. Could—"

"It wasn't a request, Jade." He's frowning.

I follow him into the living room, where Mrs. McCall is perched on the edge of one of the couches. I sit across from her. This isn't good.

"We got a concerning call," Mr. McCall says.

"A call? From who?" I ask. My mouth is dry.

"The police," Mrs. McCall tells me.

"The police?" I echo.

"Some special task force," she explains. "The officer said that a user with an ISP address in our house was engaging with someone on TikTok who's being monitored for illegal activities." She raises her eyebrows. "It wasn't me or Dad, which leaves you, Jade." My jaw falls open, but no words come out. "I thought we agreed to no social media. And aside from that, what are you mixed up in? Who's this person you're talking to?"

Shit! "I— It isn't like that," I say. "I was only goofing around. I stayed away from school friends' accounts—which is what I thought the social media ban is really about. I was just scrolling out of boredom." Obviously, Agent Meadows was right—that poster was a legit troll.

Mr. McCall looks ready to combust. "So you thought that friends from school were off limits, but hey, criminals should be fine?"

"No! I saw this random conspiracy theory post and left a comment under it. I didn't think it was a big deal." My voice scales high toward the end. "I'm sorry. I won't do it again. I swear, I had no idea the user was shady. Absolutely none."

Mr. McCall sighs.

"We're sorry to do this," Mrs. McCall says, "but we've taken your laptop, and I need your phone also. You asked for greater freedom, Jade, but trust has to be maintained once it's extended.

You went back on your word."

Mrs. McCall holds out her hand, and I reluctantly give up the phone, relieved I placed a pass code on it. There's a good chance they'll ask me to unlock it, the way they're acting, but I'll have to say no. They *can't* see the messages between me and LC or dig through my search history. I'll deal with whatever level of pissed they get if it comes to that. (Luckily, I'm pretty sure I remembered to erase my browser history on the laptop.)

This is a huge-ass problem, though. I won't be able to contact anyone—not Ryan, not Ava, not Agent Meadows. I pray Ryan got that last text I sent asking him to come over. I *need* to tell him what happened, and I *need* a link to the world outside Jade's house. I can get him to grab me a prepaid phone, at least.

After chewing me out, Mr. McCall disappears into the office and Mrs. McCall goes upstairs, so I follow my impulse to go to the game room. I'm so on edge that the only thing that might settle me is playing piano.

For a few seconds, it works. The muffled quiet that comes from putting on the headphones makes me feel separated from all the shit going on, and my hands on the keys send a sense of calm washing through me. But a moment after I start playing, my index finger strikes the wrong key. A discordant G note rings out. I start to play again—try to get lost in the music. I can't; it's impossible to focus. My mind is rebelling, wondering if Ryan is on his way, worrying about everything Meadows said, wondering about her piercing . . .

Eventually, I give up, just sit in the game room while I wait on

Ryan. However, that doesn't work either. The space is too quiet, my worries even louder inside my head.

A horn beeps. I turn to look out one of the floor-to-ceiling windows for Ryan's Jeep. But the dim driveway is empty. The horn must've sounded from the street. Dusk yields to full night a short while later, and the darkness that falls is disturbing after everything Meadows said earlier. I can't stop my mind from wandering to the criminals who developed the tech. The TikTok post. My comment.

I stare past the driveway, out at the street, imagining somebody might be out there watching me. There are no blinds or curtains downstairs and so much glass around the room—so much glass around the entire house—that it'd be easy to see in. I might as well be in a fishbowl. Every shadow that's cast outside, every gust of evening wind that kicks up, every sound of a car door slamming makes me feel like the danger is getting closer. It's all too much.

I hurry out of the game room. Upstairs, I lock the door to Jade's room behind me. We haven't even had dinner yet, but I climb into bed and curl into a ball. Close my eyes and pray again that Ryan is on his way. Before I doze off into a fitful sleep, the last thought I have is a vision of me, older, in the future, still wearing Jade's face.

I'm managing to eat what small amount of a tofu scramble I can the next morning when the doorbell rings. The display panel on the wall shows Ryan standing on the doorstep. I tear from the kitchen to the front door.

But Mrs. McCall is already there. "Jade can't have company right now," she tells Ryan. "And don't even try to argue," she says to me.

"I won't," I say to her. To Ryan, I rush out, "Don't be mad I'm not texting! They took my phone." I need him to know that much, at least.

Ryan looks between me and Jade's mom, his forehead creased. "I'm very sorry, Mrs. McCall," he says. "I'll go." He stares at me intently, briefly glances upward, then looks at me again. It's as if he's trying to silently communicate something, but I have no idea what it is. "See you later, Jade," he says, and turns to leave.

More trapped and isolated than ever, I retreat upstairs again and scream into a pillow to get out my frustration. I need a plan, but I can't come up with one unless I clear my head and calm down.

Before I can do anything, there's a *thud* against the window. I sit up, my heart skipping a beat.

THUD!

The blinds are still drawn, so I can't see what it is. I grip the comforter. Clearly, I'm channeling a white girl in a horror movie, because I ease off the bed and walk *toward* the damn noise, telling myself it's probably a branch on the giant tree beside the house knocking against the glass. Still, I grab Jade's massive chem textbook off the desk on my way past and hold it at the ready.

As I reach the window, I count to three, gathering my courage, then boss up and open the blinds. *Fuck!* I jump back, drop the textbook. A face is staring at me through the glass. I'm two seconds away from yelling at the top of my lungs for the McCalls when I realize it's Ryan.

"You scared the heck out of me!" I whisper, after pushing open the window. My body is buzzing with adrenaline. I look toward the door to make sure it's closed.

"My bad," he says, clambering awkwardly from a tree branch into the room. "I didn't mean to scare you."

I gape at him—and then at the tree. "You climbed that?!"

"Yeah. I was trying to tell you I'd come up that way at the door—then remembered you aren't Jade, so you wouldn't know about our secret way to hang out when she's grounded." He glances back at the tree. "Haven't done it in a while. Either the branch is weaker or I'm bulkier."

I laugh. I can't help it. "If you and Jade were an item, this whole thing would be cute but hella cliché."

"I'm actually a die-hard *Romeo and Juliet* fan, so I'm not insulted." He grins. His smile really should be illegal because it short-circuits my brain every time. "Sorry I couldn't come last night," he says as we sit on the bed. "I was at a thing with my parents that I couldn't ditch. Why'd the McCalls take your phone? And how'd it go with the FBI lady?"

My meeting with Meadows in the diner feels like it was *days* ago; I've learned so much since then.

"Bear with me," I say. "It's a lot." And I start in, telling him everything that Agent Meadows told me at the diner; how I was nervous to give my family's address, so she had me track LC with

RSP; and how I saw her piercing in the car, but she explained it away.

"Damn," says Ryan once I finish. "That *is* a lot. So, what do we do next?"

I shrug, then roughly wipe my eyes, tears of frustration and fear that I've been holding back finally falling. Ryan's arms lock around me. Before I even consciously make the decision, I hug him back, lay my head against his chest. For a moment, we just sit there, our breath syncing up.

"You draw?" he asks.

"Huh?"

He points at the sketch of a woman beside us on the floor—must have fallen out of Jade's chem book. "No," I say, picking it up. "LC drew it. I don't suppose you've ever seen this lady before?"

Ryan shakes his head. "Nope."

I set the drawing aside and wipe my eyes.

Time to focus.

"Can I use your phone?" I ask.

Ryan hands it to me, but I don't use it for what I have in mind straightaway. I take some time to work out how I'm going to play this. Because the thing is, evil or not, LC's the one person who has what I want: my body. I need to make sure she's not going to take off with it and need to assure her I won't give her location to Meadows. Which means I also need to convince her of a few lies of my own. Because if I've figured one thing, it's this: LC played me; I've got to play her, however I can. *That's how I take my life back.*

When I call her, LC answers on the second ring.

"Tess is dangerous. Stay away from her," she hisses the minute she hears my voice.

"That's what Agent Meadows claims about you," I respond evenly.

"That woman is *not* FBI," LC spits.

"I saw her badge and read an article about her being a community hero online," I say. "What do you mean she isn't FBI?"

"I promise, any article you saw was planted by her," LC says. "Tess is smart enough to fabricate whatever she needs to sell her lies."

Like you are! I manage not to snap. Instead, I reply plainly, "I feel that way about you, so . . . why should I believe you? Especially when *you* hurt me already." I pause, then add, "Really bad. And not only with the swap. I thought we were actually best friends." I let my voice reveal how gutted I am. *You catch more flies with honey than vinegar.* It's a corny Dad saying—and hopefully it applies here. Nobody is completely soulless, right? There has to be *some* way to reach LC.

She's quiet for a second. "That's fair," she says. I widen my eyes at Ryan, stunned she uttered it. To even get that much out of her, my tactic must be working.

"The lie Tess told *me* was that she was a therapist who wanted to help me," LC continues. "She hurt me instead."

"I can't know what to believe for sure without the full story or some proof."

"I get that," she says, then remains silent.

A moment ago, she sounded like she finally wanted to tell me her story, and now she's acting like she can't say shit. What the hell is up with her?

"Meadows told me that you lost your parents," I say. "If that's true, it's terrible, and I'm sorry. I can't even imagine not having my family. Everyone deserves a stable home." I pause. No response. "I *know* you have a good heart, despite what you did. Like I *know* I saw part of the real you while we were friends. Whatever your reasons are for swapping us, you've got to see how you've now taken my family away from me, the same way yours was taken. They're lost to me forever—unless we switch back."

I squeeze the phone, wait for her to respond. She still doesn't say anything. Only breathes heavily.

"*LC!*" I plead. "What's your endgame, honestly? Did you do this to me and Jade just to make others feel your pain? Do you plan to keep hurting people forever? Living this way seems really sad. And lonely. I can help you do something different, help you get whatever you want, if you know what it is. We can figure it out together. I swear. *Please*, give me and Jade our lives back. You *aren't* this cruel. You can't be!"

"*Megan* . . ." LC's voice wobbles. I hold my breath. "I—"

I don't get a chance to hear what she's going to say. Because just at that moment, there's a quick knock at my bedroom door, and Mrs. McCall saying, "Jade?" And before I can stop her, she's entered the room.

Twenty-One

I'm sitting on the floor of Jade's room, staring at a piece of paper in a spiral notebook where I've written *Can we talk using RSP?*, wondering how long I should remain here looking at it to be sure that LC has seen it. Of course, Mrs. McCall freaked the fuck out when she discovered Ryan had snuck in and ordered him out. But right before I had to hang up and return his phone, I told LC, "Use your RSP!" And I'm praying she'll get what I meant. Because there's no way I'm seeing Ryan again anytime in this century, which means I have no phone access to communicate with her.

I stare at my notebook page for a couple of minutes, giving LC extra time to tune in to her RSP, see the *Can we talk* message, and then write a response to me. After the minutes pass, I grab the ring box with my violet hair. I hold the strand and brace for the wave of vertigo. My heart leaps when I'm seeing out of LC's eyes. She's in my bedroom, looking at a MacBook screen, on which she has typed: Yes.

I put down the hair and take a moment to shake off the slight RSP dizziness. Then I write:

What were you about to say before I hung up?

I stare at my words for a long minute—giving LC time to read it—before picking up the hair and tuning into my RSP again.

The cursor on LC's screen starts moving beneath her initial response.

Body swapping isn't the only thing Tess's technology can do. It can be used to mess with people's brains. To remove memories—that sort of thing. Tess used me as a lab rat to see just how far she can play God. She stole my memories from when my parents were alive. I can't recall their faces, their names, or any details about them, or anything we ever did together. My childhood is a big fucking blank.

Whoa. That's terrible if it's true. And I can't entirely squash pity for LC this time—even though logically I know parts of this could be a lie.

I continue reading:

It's why I haven't run farther away from Tess. I keep trying to find a way to take my memories back—they're stored on a drive in her lab. But now I see that it's impossible. Even if I break into Tess's lab safely, the memories are in a secure area, which needs a retina scan for access. I've tried to find a way around it or a way to disable it.

I'm finally admitting there isn't any way. There's nothing I can do short of luring Tess to unlock the lab herself, and I cannot—under any circumstances—be in that lab with Tess ever again. The woman is a real-life evil scientist who is narcissistic and sadistic as fuck beneath the bogus niceness. Who knows what she'll do to me to make me pay for running if she gets me hooked up again in her lab and uses the Cogitec on me?

LC continues typing. However, I pause on the unfamiliar word. "Cogitec," I murmur. Setting the violet hair on the desk for a second, I write the term in my notebook while it's fresh so I'll get the spelling right. My electronics are gone, but I've got to find a way to look it up, even if research is risky. I pick up the hair, refocus on the MacBook screen, and read the rest of what LC typed.

I promise I always meant to make it right with you and Jade. I only made the switches to stay ahead of Tess as she hunted me down. I needed to block her from tracking me with RSP while remaining near enough to her lab. I was gonna eventually get my memories and swap us into our correct bodies. But I'm willing to let those memories go. It's less of a risk to just give up, run farther away, and vanish for good—in my real body. I hate feeling like I'm the same monster as Tess, and I want to give you and Jade your lives back. The problem is, I don't have enough Cogitec equipment left for two swaps. I only have enough for one. We need to get more from Tess. You need to steal it from her. She always carries some on her, and you're close to her already since she's using you to track me.

I scowl. Of course that's what this is about. Now I get the real reason that LC is suddenly so eager to explain herself. She needs me to get her more Cogitec while she stays far away from Meadows. And she's become desperate enough for more that she's willing to trade me my body for it.

Still, while there's no way in hell that I'll take anything LC says as truth without indisputable proof—if there's any chance that she'll hold up her end of the deal and give me and Jade our bodies back, I have to at least see where it goes. Especially when relying on Meadows isn't a sure bet, either. If Meadows *is* an agent, like she claims, then she's one whose target keeps eluding her— no guarantee LC won't keep doing that. And if Meadows *isn't* an agent, like *LC* claims . . . well, there's no way she actually means to help me.

LC just handed me what might be my best chance to save myself. I just have to accept the risk that if I get her more Cogitec, she might vanish *for good* in my body, with enough hardware to switch several more times whenever she needs to.

My head spins. I don't know who or what to believe. And yet I've still got to make a choice. Before I do, I write to LC again:

If you're being real, tell me how the swaps are actually done. How does Cogitec work?

Text starts appearing on the laptop screen:

Think of how a computer and USB flash drive work

together. The person is like the computer, and Cogitec is like the flash drive. The hole in your neck itself provides the pathway for Cogitec to plug into your nervous system. Imagine it as the access route. The barbell I pierced you with is really a needlelike drive with a microchip inside, the exact way a USB drive has a storage chip in it. A copy of your entire consciousness was automatically uploaded to the microchip when you got pierced. Microchips can be swapped between people, the same way you can remove a flash drive from one computer and plug it into another. When that happens, the consciousness on the newly inserted microchip overrides the previous one.

LC hits the basics of what I'd already guessed, so her explanation rings true.

What about the drug you gave me? I ask. *Is that part of it?*

It takes a second before she starts writing again.

No, it doesn't have to be. That was just something to put you out for a few hours so you wouldn't know what was happening. You can swap without it.

Reading that, and remembering our night at Nathan's party, old feelings of anger and hurt resurge. But I push them aside. The important thing is that I now know that if this *does* reach the point of another swap, I won't be helpless and unconscious again. That's something, at least.

So, I've gotten my answers about how this was done to me. The only thing left is to choose what I'll do with the knowledge.

I need to listen to that fundamental, truest part of myself—the only voice that's even remotely dependable, I'm finally learning. It offers up another one of dad's truisms: *The devil you know is better than the devil you don't.* I guess with LC and Meadows, that means the devil I've known longer is better than the devil I just met. (That logic might be faulty as shit, but I'm desperate too.)

Where would Meadows keep the Cogitec? I ask LC.

A metal case like the one I have should be in her trunk.

I sit with that, unsure which possibility is scarier: me stealing from a cop with a gun or a criminal with a gun.

I swallow both fears and tell LC:

I'll steal the Cogitec and help you escape Meadows if you stick to your word about me and Jade. But I'm coming up with the plan for how I deliver you the Cogitec and how the swaps get done.

I want to be in charge of that part in order to control what happens—and minimize LC's ability to go back on our deal—as much as possible.

Let me think on the plan. We'll use RSP again in one hour, I scrawl to LC.

I place the violet strand of hair safely back into the ring box and cut our connection—on my side, at least. I sit and think for a good bit of time. Coming up with a solid plan on my own proves a hell of a lot easier said than done. There are so many variables, after all. So much that can go wrong. Too much danger from all sides.

But then I have one wild idea that could work. If I can get in touch with Jade.

I'm writing the whole thing down for LC when I hear the doorbell downstairs. Could it be Ryan again? I roll my chair to the door, crack it open, and listen to the faint voices. One of them is Meadows's. I stiffen. *Why is she here?!*

Meadows's voice carries upstairs. "I'm a caseworker from the Georgia Division of Family and Children Services," she lies. "I'm sorry to interrupt your day, but welfare checks after a child runs away are mandatory. I'd like to check in with Jade, personally, to make sure everything is fine. Is she home?"

Mrs. McCall tells Meadows that I'm in my room and that she'll take her up to me. I ease the door shut and roll back to the desk.

It makes sense that Meadows wouldn't tell them she's an FBI agent, since Cogitec and my involvement are secret. And yet, as footsteps crack against the stairs, my gut insists something is wrong.

The steps cease. A light knock sounds. "Jade? There's a social worker here to visit with you," Mrs. McCall says. "A routine check-in. Your case was handed off to her from the Atlanta folks. Can you come downstairs to the office? She requested to interview you without me and your dad present, if that's all right?"

I have an urge to shout, *No!* But that's silly, when I just agreed to steal Cogitec from Meadows. It doesn't matter who or what she is or why she's here. I need access to her car.

"One second!" I call. "I'll meet her downstairs."

"Why aren't you picking up your phone?" Meadows asks in a low voice once Mrs. McCall leaves us alone in the office. She sounds genuinely concerned instead of furious.

"The . . . the McCalls took it," I stammer.

A look of relief crosses her face. "Parents can do the most annoying things. Right? Don't worry; this will be over super soon. Have you managed to check in on LC again?"

Her manner is so kind. But I already know it's impossible to tell if somebody is foul by how they act. I charge ahead with the plan I just came up with, even though I haven't been able to talk to Jade first, but hopefully that won't matter.

"I've been keeping track of LC like you asked," I say. "I last saw her in a car. She was following Google Maps to Brighthaven. I don't know why she'd go see Jade, but if we go now, we can meet her there."

"Brighthaven?" Meadows says, looking surprised. "Okay. That will work."

"Do you think you can come up with an excuse for Jade's parents?" I ask. "They won't want me disappearing with someone they don't know."

She nods. "No problem. Are you ready?"

As she asks, I suddenly realize it's been almost exactly an hour since I was in touch with LC—she'll be waiting to use our RSP.

"I'm going to get a jacket real quick for the drive," I tell

Meadows, heading for the office door. I open it hurriedly and step out of the room, not giving her the chance to object.

Once I'm back in Jade's room, I grab a tube of lipstick out of the vanity's drawer. I write on the mirror: *Meet us at the group home ASAP. Wait INSIDE with Jade. Trust me.*

I stare at it for as long as I can without making Meadows suspicious about what I'm doing up here. Then I grab a jacket and the ring box with the violet hair and head out, praying that the girl who steps into this bedroom next is the real Jade McCall—and not me.

Twenty-Two

On the highway, I repeatedly go over my plan in my head—every little detail—to be sure there aren't snags that I didn't think of before. Of course, there are things I can't control—like LC figuring out how to get into the group home without Jade knowing the plan. But if there's one thing I know about LC, it's that she'll find a way.

As I'm mentally rehearsing what to say to get the Cogitec from Meadows, I realize she's just driven past the exit for Decatur Falls, the small town where the group home is.

"We're making a detour first," Meadows explains.

"Where are we going? Why aren't we headed straight to Brighthaven?"

"Hold on," she says as her phone rings. "This is about the case."

I go cold when she takes the call before giving me an answer. I have no idea where we're headed—that's definitely a snag!

I calm down a bit when the conversation she's having makes

her sound like an actual FBI agent. She speaks to someone briefly about having located Lainey Carter, who she'll be apprehending soon. "Lainey is waiting in Decatur Falls," she tells the person. "I'm headed there right after an important stop by the office. I'll keep you updated."

My anxiety doesn't fully uncoil, though, because I remember LC's warning—how Meadows hooked her up to some computer there and stole her memories. "What's at your office?" I ask when she's off the phone.

Meadows tells me readily: "The tech for the swaps."

Her explanation would seem solid enough if LC hadn't already said she keeps some Cogitec on her. I wring my hands in my lap. Again, I wonder, what the hell should I believe? *Who* should I believe?

I scramble to think of a way out of the car in case I need to escape. I stare out the window, imagining what would happen if I jumped out at the speed we're going. If I were extremely lucky and didn't kill myself, how would I get away from Meadows on foot, though?

It becomes a battle not to hyperventilate when we cross state lines and pass a bright blue and green sign that says: *Welcome to Florida. The Sunshine State.*

We exit the highway when we reach Jacksonville, where my football-obsessed UGA-alumnus Mom drags Dad, Sophie, and me to every year for the Florida-Georgia rivalry game. I relax by a degree at the familiarity of my surroundings. Things could be much worse; I could've found myself in a strange place that I had no hope of knowing how to navigate.

The Volvo finally stops in front of a small office building. Meadows rolls down the window and presses her thumb to a fingerprint scanner outside of a large black gate. After a beep, the gate slides open and Meadows drives through. The high security isn't lost on me. I'm unsure if it's a good sign or bad one. A concealed FBI base of operations for undercover agents would have strict security. But so might a secret location where a criminal does shady shit.

The entrance to the low brick building requires the same thumb scan. The building itself is nondescript, giving no hint of whether I'm walking into a real-life mad scientist's base camp or not. The lobby is bare and empty; no one in sight except me and Meadows.

"Can I wait in the car?" I ask, failing to keep my voice steady.

The way she ignores me raises the hairs on the back of my neck. *Should I try to run?*

As if sensing my debate, Meadows subtly adjusts her gun as she leads me down a narrow, dimly lit hallway with security cameras positioned along the ceiling. I flick a look upward at a camera we pass by. *Wonder if security guards are watching the feeds and if there's anybody around who might help if Meadows tries to hurt me.*

"This is where the magic begins," Meadows says, opening a door to reveal a large modern room with a glass-top desk, computer, two chairs, a small sofa, no windows. Three degrees in psychology hang on the wall: a bachelor's from Florida State, a master's from University of Miami, and a doctorate from Yale. Looks like Meadows is one of those FBI agents who study behavioral psych. There are agents who have that exact job on cop shows.

But then Meadows turns to me and says, "This is how things are going to go. You and I will swap bodies so that you'll be inside mine and I'll be inside Jade's."

What?! Swap into Meadows's *body?!*

This woman is absolutely no FBI agent.

I back away, but Meadows touches her gun and warns, "Don't move."

"I'll do whatever you want!" I cry, freezing. "Just, please, don't hurt me!" I have no idea why she wants to swap with me. But I do *not* want to swap with her—being inside Jade's body is downright normal compared to the idea of being inside *Meadows's*!

"That's good to hear," she replies plainly. "You'll be just fine as long as you do *exactly* what I say. LC is creating a lot of inconveniences for me, and you're going to help me finally get my hands on her so I can put a stop to it. She'll lower her guard around you, of course; that's why I'm meeting her at Brighthaven in *your* body."

No.

No!

I fight to stop shaking. Things have spun so far out of my control. Why did I ever believe I could manage this? Why did I ever imagine I could protect myself against Meadows if she turned out to be a criminal, like LC said she was? LC certainly couldn't. Her story was *real*, and all she could do to remain safe from Meadows was run and keep running.

"LC will know something is off," I say quickly. "When you show up as Jade, she's gonna notice that you don't act or talk like I would. She knows me too well. We hung out nonstop for three months. It's not like tricking someone who doesn't even know body swapping exists. She'll know!" I'm trembling harder by the time I finish.

Tess's face is cruelly blank as she reaches for me. I don't dodge her quick enough. The sleeve of her blazer catches on an earring that rips from my ear, causing a sharp dart of pain, and then her cold fingers dig into the nape of my neck. "If you move, I *will* kill you," she says, voice calm. She yanks a small piercing gun from an inside pocket, clicks a button on the side, presses it against my barbell.

"Please, no!" I beg.

I brace for the bite of pain from the piercing gun.

There is none.

But the world dims, goes murky. Energy floods out of me like I'm a battery that's been drained. I sag in Tess's hold, too weak to fight anymore. She shifts me onto one of the nearby chairs.

"Wh—what did you to me?" I heave, words sluggish.

Tess grins smugly and tells me: "I just copied every bit of data inside your brain onto a microchip in here." She waves the piercing gun. "Isn't it awe-inspiring? The body clings to whatever consciousness occupies it until a new one overrides it. It took a number of trials to perfect a total override that stuck, but eventually I got there. You should be honored, Megan. You're witnessing firsthand something truly innovative and miraculous that will transform the globe. By helping me get LC, you're ensuring Cogitec makes its way out into the world, and that means *you're* also playing a role in something huge. Something that will *change lives* and *save them*."

Meadows presses the Cogitec gun against the back of her own neck. And if I'm understanding everything right, she's going to download her own consciousness onto a microchip like she just did with mine. As I have the thought, she wobbles, sags, as if her legs might give out. But even if I had the energy, I don't have time to take advantage of it—to knock her down and grab her gun and take control. She shakes off the lethargy almost immediately— maybe because she's swapped multiple times before—and grabs me again and presses the gun to my neck.

In the next breath, the world blinks out. I don't tumble into darkness—everything is just blank.

My surroundings re-blink into focus . . . and I'm in Meadows's body.

I glance down and flinch at hands that are white. My breath turns ragged with horror when I reach up and touch stringy hair and a super-narrow nose. Then there's the high heels pinching small feet, the snug-fitting blazer covering a smaller chest. Not to mention my vision itself—I see everything around me sharper than I'm used to with Jade.

Meadows heads toward the door. My mind reels at seeing Jade's body, *which I was just in*, being operated by somebody else. It feels like not existing as an actual person but as some insub- stantial, artificial thing that can be plucked from one casing and plopped into a new one at a whim.

I stand up, but I'm off-balance on the high heels and have to steady myself.

"Don't bother yelling for help," Meadows says, opening the door. "The office is soundproof."

With that, the door slams shut behind her.

Twenty-Three

I stare at the office door, shell-shocked. It takes some time to come to my senses. Finally, I kick off Meadows's heels and try to open the door. When it won't budge, I twist the lock on the handle, already knowing she'll have done something to keep me from escaping. Sure enough, an electronic voice rings out: "Manual lock is disabled. Please use the remote app."

Shit. Shit. Shit.

I don't care that she said the room is soundproof. I scream. I scream and scream and scream, banging on the door. I do it until I'm hoarse. But no one comes.

Heart pounding, I avert my eyes from the pale hands curled into fists. Fresh panic engulfs me. Even if I get out of this room, I'll still be trapped in Meadows's body. I *do not* want to stay like this! Being inside some sinister white lady's body is fucking disturbing on a *Get Out* type of level!

You cannot lose it, Megan. Pull it together and think.

I take a deep breath and remember a vital truth: *No matter what body I'm in, I'm not Meadows. I am Megan.* What I look like on the outside means shit. Nothing and nobody can strip *who* I am. I need to hold on to that so I can keep my head enough to find a way through this.

Closing my eyes, I center myself by remembering the Brahms concerto I've been learning. Every new note grounds me more firmly. I may be terrified, but I've already withstood so much and gotten through it. I'm not used to thinking of myself as intrinsically strong or confident or courageous, but when I think back over all the wild crap I've dealt with, and all the times I've had to keep it together despite being petrified, it's pretty unbelievable. And hella . . . well . . . *fierce*! All of that is Megan. And Megan is abso-fucking-lutely going to get out of this. *And*, I promise myself, *not only that; I'm going to make sure it never happens to anyone else.*

I pat down Meadows's pockets for *something* that could help. But they're empty. No keys. No phone. (No surprise.)

I try the computer. If I can get it unlocked, I can DM Ryan and Ava to call the real cops. It's password protected, of course. Remembering the thumb scanners Meadows used, I scan the keyboard, mouse, and monitor for anything that could function like that.

Nothing.

I'm about to tear the whole room apart—search all the drawers and cabinets and shelves—when something gold glints on the carpet a few feet from the desk. It's an earring—the one that was pulled out of my ear during my tussle with Meadows.

All of a sudden I realize: *RSP*. I was wearing the earring when I was in Jade's body, which means it will let me see through Jade's eyes—the body that Meadows is in now. It's not much, but it's something. I can get a sense of what's going on and where she is.

I pick it up, grit past the moment of vertigo, and tune in to my RSP.

The first thing I see through Jade's eyes is the barrel of a gun pointing straight at Jade as she drives Meadows's Volvo. I instinctively flinch at the sight. The gun is being held by "Megan." Whoever is in my body is sitting by herself in the Volvo's back seat. LC is up front next to Jade, clearly terrified. Whoever is in my body must be forcing Jade to drive somewhere at gunpoint. But is that really Jade, or is it someone else? And who is in *my* body?

I'm so confused that I have to set down the earring so I can think straight.

Who is who?

The last I knew, Meadows was in *Jade*'s body, LC was in *my* body, and Jade was in *LC*'s body.

Meadows said she was going to use Jade's body to lure LC into a trap. But "Jade" is now driving while being held at gunpoint. Does that mean Meadows failed, and LC—still in my body—is holding the gun on her? If so, where is she making Meadows drive to? It can't be the lab. LC said she'd never come near this place— and she certainly wouldn't come with Meadows. Regardless of their destination, I want, so badly, to believe that LC did turn the tables on her.

I pick up the earring again to see if I catch something outside the car that'll clue me in to where they're headed. It takes some time, but eventually I glimpse the *Welcome to Florida* sign. I don't know if I want to sigh in relief or cry out in horror. On one hand, now I know their destination: they must be coming to the lab. On the other hand, that has to mean the person holding the gun is really Meadows.

Of course it's Meadows. *Of course* she somehow kept the upper hand!

I stay levelheaded, don't let my mind whirlpool again at the realizations that Meadows now pilots my real body and that they're near. *This is good. Meadows isn't leaving me here to rot and die. And once she comes, I'll be ready for her.*

I've got one chance to get all three of us—me, Jade, and LC—out of Meadows's grasp.

LC SHOULD'VE SUSPECTED a setup the moment "Megan" showed up at Brighthaven. There was something off about her right from the start. But LC didn't figure it out until the gun was inches from her face.

At first, she believed Megan's story. That she'd overpowered Tess and taken her car. That she had all the Cogitec they needed, and after swapping, LC could take the car and drive as far as she wanted. LC and Megan snuck Jade out of the group home, and Megan led them to Tess's Volvo. Once in the car, they'd done the swaps—LC naively assuming they were all now in their right bodies. That some of her wrongs had been righted.

LC's joy was short-lived. Megan grabbed a gun out of the back seat. LC knew immediately who Megan really was before Tess smugly dropped the revelation herself and threatened to shoot LC and Jade if they didn't do exactly as she ordered.

Now Tess keeps the gun on Jade as Jade drives them to the

lab. LC hates Tess with all the loathing a person can possess. Her hands itch to reach into the back seat and wrap themselves around Tess's damn throat. Or shoot her dead and be safe from her for good—she deserves either. Deserves more, actually. But even if she dared make an attempt while Tess has the gun, Tess is piloting Megan's body, and Megan doesn't deserve that.

Jade swerves a bit, clearly too nervous to drive well.

Tess says: "Calm down. Megan's waiting at the lab. We'll swap her into her right body too, then I'll hook you all up and remove your memories of everything involving me and Cogitec. This is all to keep you safe. Nothing bad will happen if you do as I say."

"Don't believe her," LC snaps.

Tess, perched in the middle of the back seat, points the gun at LC, a clear warning to shut up.

Dread keeps LC in a chokehold the rest of the drive. She doesn't trust for a second that Tess will do what she promises. It's not in Tess's nature to simply let three convenient test subjects go. She will do worse things to them than just erase their memories of Cogitec if she gets them hooked up in her lab. LC doesn't know exactly what Tess will do—how much of the information in their brains she'll erase—but nothing would surprise her. Tess may not technically kill them, but is it so different if she removes everything that defines them? What would remain? LC has just started to build back a sense of self. She refuses to let it be taken away.

Twenty-Four

I keep hold of the earring, tracking them the remainder of the drive. Finally, I glimpse the parking lot outside the lab building. They're here. I hide to the side of the door, my back pressed against the wall, pulse pounding in my ears. A minute later, the lock audibly clicks open. The handle turns.

I take one second to swallow my nerves—don't let myself think too hard about what comes next. I remain still as LC and Jade enter. Then as Meadows—in my body—steps into the room, I throw myself at her. We crash to the ground. Someone screams. The gun skitters across the floor. I landed on top of her, and I know I'm going to hate myself for it later, but I shift my weight to the hand that's in the soft cast. Meadows hollers out. I wince, as if feeling the pain myself, but stay planted and grab the handcuffs sticking out of Meadows's jeans pocket.

"Help me restrain her!" I cry to LC and Jade, indescribably spooked that this evil-ass white woman is in my damn body.

The girl I visited at Brighthaven drops down beside me. "We swapped back into our real bodies," LC quickly explains.

LC helps me drag Meadows to a heavy-looking cabinet near the desk. I cuff her to one of the cabinet's legs, ignoring her threats and demands to be let go. (And compartmentalizing *extremely* hard, since doing this to my own body is hella unnerving.)

I stare Meadows down. "Don't bother screaming. Nobody will hear you, right?"

She turns a bright shade of red as I pat her pockets, finding a handcuff key that I shove in my blazer pocket. I grab the gun—it's risky to leave it anywhere around Meadows, handcuffed or not. My fingers close around the cool metal clumsily. I've never held a weapon before. I point it at the floor and keep my fingers far away from the trigger. The last thing we need is for it to be discharged, even by accident. "Do you know if there are keys to the desk drawers around here?" I ask LC. "I want to lock up the gun."

She frowns. "Why? We need it." She glances at Meadows.

I shake my head. "Too much chance one of us'll get hurt."

"I agree with Megan," Jade says. She's been standing near the door, hands clasped together tight.

LC doesn't look happy about it, but she doesn't argue further. She finds the desk key easily, knowing where Meadows keeps stuff from the time she spent here.

"Tess left some Cogitec in her car," LC tells me once the gun's locked away. "One of us can go get it; the other can stay and watch Tess. After that, we can get you back into your body. And Tess . . ." LC pauses. "Maybe we'll upload her into her own body, too. *Or maybe we won't.*"

The stone-faced manner she drops the last bit makes me certain she isn't joking. I hadn't even thought of that possibility. Meadows doesn't deserve to get away with anything she's done—she'll always be dangerous. And I do want to stop her from destroying lives. But what LC suggested is pseudo murder. Or outright murder, possibly?

"If a person who's had their consciousness relocated to a microchip never gets reuploaded to a new body, what ultimately happens to that person?"

She glares at Meadows. "I don't know. But Dr. Meadows loves a convenient, *available* test case. Don't you?"

Meadows blanches. "After we swap, I'll let you all go," she tells me. "I won't hook you up, erase any memories, or do anything else!" she says frantically to LC.

LC smirks. "Like I'd ever believe you."

"Hook me up, then! Erase my memories of you three, like I did with your past. You can do that and be safe!"

"That was the *wrong* thing to say," LC responds coldly.

"No," I inform Meadows. "You don't get to control how this ends. LC is right. You can't be trusted."

"What do you want to do, then, Megan?" Jade asks, looking between LC and Meadows skittishly. She's keeping them both in her view, and I don't blame her. "I understand if you don't trust LC to go get the equipment and perform the swaps. I'll do it for you. You know you can trust me."

I shake my head.

I open my mouth to speak, and then hesitate. Do I really have the guts to say what I'm going to say?

"I'm staying in Meadows's body for now." The words come out strong. Confident.

"You're what?!" LC cries. "Why the fuck would you do that?!"

Obviously, the simpler, smartest thing to do would be to swap back into my own body as soon as possible. That's all I've wanted since the night of Nathan's party! It's what I've prayed for. What I've been scared to death would never happen. And after taking what belongs to me back, I could leave Meadows's fate in LC's hands. Let LC be the one to decide whether to upload her consciousness back into her body or let it exist in the limbo of a microchip. It wouldn't be *me* doing it, so *I* wouldn't technically become a killer.

But . . . where would that leave LC? How would that ending save Meadows's first victim? It would liberate her in a way, sure. Meadows wouldn't be able to hurt her ever again. But how would it affect the rest of LC's life to know that she'd been responsible for essentially murdering someone, no matter how evil that person was? *Who* and *what* would LC become?

I shouldn't give a damn. I should just take my body, cut out, and leave LC to the mess that started with her and Meadows. After all, LC has wrongs to pay for, too. But I don't think I want her to pay by further wrecking her own sense of self and dropping deeper into a seriously dark place. In fact . . . I realize . . . I don't want LC to pay anymore. Whatever else she may be, LC's a fellow Black girl who suffered trauma too. In fact, that's likely a big part of why Meadows targeted her and thought she could use her like a lab rat, co-opt her body and mind, and strip away precious bits with no consequences. Too much of society has a way of not giving a fuck about us. Of turning away and letting us be hurt. I won't perpetuate that. I won't leave LC so clearly damaged and screwed over if there's a way I can help her heal and live a less bleak future. Also, it may be wildly illogical, but there's still that tiny part of me that believes in the LC I thought I knew. The one I loved.

So if it means risking a little extra time in the body of this evil woman to see if I can help her, I've decided that it's worth it. And it's satisfying to know that it'll be possible because of the power that Tess herself handed me.

"I have to go do something important," I tell Jade. "Can you keep Meadows in check for a while? I'll be back as soon as I can and explain everything later."

Jade seems to get that I don't want to say more in front of Meadows. "Yeah. I've got it," she automatically says.

Next, I turn to LC, step in close, and whisper so only she hears, "The Cogitec lab is here too, right? The one that needs a retina scan for access?"

LC swallows; her tenuous hope is clear.

"You know how to get there?" I ask.

She nods.

I grab her hand and we rush out into the hallway.

I've got two things to accomplish before I can finally be myself again.

One: get LC her childhood memories back.

Two: talk her out of keeping Meadows unplugged.

Twenty-Five

"Thank you," LC says as she leads us down a corridor. We're walking as fast as we can without actually running. "You didn't have to do this."

"It's the right thing to do," I say quietly.

Footsteps echo before either of us can say anything else. We freeze when a security guard rounds the corner. *Shit*.

"Your badges aren't visible," he says as he nears. "Can I see them?"

I force myself to relax and appear unconcerned. I make a show of patting down my blazer and pants pockets. "I must've left mine behind," I state.

"How about yours?" he asks LC.

I bite my cheeks as she stuffs hands into her jeans pockets like she's checking for one. "I'm sorry," she says, following my lead. "We both must've left them back in the car."

The guard scowls and rests a hand on his radio. "I'll need to walk with you outside."

Just then, I remember who I look like. "Excuse me?" I say in an icy tone. "I am *Doctor* Tess Meadows, and this is my assistant. I have work to do. If you have a problem with that, we can speak to your supervisor." It's what a *Karen* would demand, and I am a white woman for the time being.

The guard smiles tightly—*phew*. "That isn't what I meant, ma'am. I'm just following policy, that's all. But I can make an exception this once."

When he steps away, I grab LC's arm and march us down the hall like I'm hella insulted. The moment we turn the corner, we pick up our pace again. We need to reach the Cogitec lab without encountering any other guards—not sure I can get us out of trouble with the Karen act twice.

"Damn!" LC grins over at me. "That was exactly how Tess would react."

I swallow a grin. We *are not* friends. Never really were. This is only me helping out a girl in a bad spot—no camaraderie is needed.

We take another corner, turning left. I'm committing our route to memory so I'll know the way back and won't need to rely on LC, in case *she* attempts something shady. Finally, she halts in front of a closed door. No sign or nameplate on it. Blank, as if what's inside is totally innocuous.

"This is the room." Her voice is an understandable mixture of hopefulness and tension.

I step in front of the retinal-scanner panel. LC presses a spot to activate it, and I open my eyes—*Tess's* eyes—wide, almost smiling at the fact that Tess underestimated me so much. *Her bad.* The lock slides open with a satisfying click.

We hurry inside and I make sure the door auto-locks behind us.

I survey the small, windowless, ice-cold room. I'd braced for it to look like some mad scientist's lab, but it's more like some sort of high-tech command center. There are two wide, cardboard-thin, slightly curved monitors on a glass desk, along with a large silver computer tower. Another four screens hanging flush on the wall. A number of sleek metal cabinets. Two ergonomic desk chairs, one with a sort of wraparound headset built in.

"I'm assuming this is the computer we need," I say, moving quickly to the desk. "Can you help me turn it on? I couldn't figure out the one in the other office."

"Hold on," LC says. She's standing in front of one of the cabinets. "Tess stores the Cogitec equipment in here. We need to get it away from her." She points to a small black panel above the handle. "I need your fingerprint."

"We should restore your memories first," I say. "Just in case. Get over here and help me!"

LC shakes her head. "Making sure Tess can't keep experimenting on people is more important." She stays planted right where she is. "Tess wasn't done with her trials when I ran. She's still fixing bugs, making it easier to use . . . seeing how far she can push its capabilities. She wants to be able to sell the tech for as high a sum as possible once she's ready."

I shudder at the thought of Cogitec existing at-large and becoming commodified. "I can't believe you actually care." The barb flies out before I can stop it.

"I promise, I get your shock—and the irony," LC mumbles. "You'll never know how sorry I am that I did the same thing to you and Jade that I hate Tess for doing to me."

I don't know what to reply to that. "Okay," I say, crossing to where she is. "Let's take it all and get this part over with already. Fast."

I get us into the cabinet, and LC grabs a large trash bag out of an unused waste container. We dump piercing guns, barbells, and small cases that contain microchips into it. "We can . . . I don't know . . . pitch this all into the river or destroy it some other way," I say once the cabinet is empty.

At the computer, LC shows me a hot corner along the bottom right side that I have to press Meadows's index and middle fingers to. That activates a retina scan that unlocks the damn thing. A home screen appears on one of the monitors, with rows of icons that mean nothing to me.

I pull up a finder window.

"She called me subject ESC0410. Try that."

I type the combination of letters and numbers into the search box. The computer begins to scan through files—the list goes on and on, so many files that I worry we might not have the time to wait for them all to be searched.

I glance at the closed door. While I'm listening to be sure I don't hear steps outside, I wonder how rotten to the core a person needs to be to offer a *kid* a place to stay under the guise of helping them, only to prey on them, reducing them to a fucking file number on a computer.

Please punish her, I beg the universe while we wait for a hit. *Make her pay.* I want that, viscerally, even if I plan to stop LC from doing it her own way.

At last, a file folder labeled *ESC0410* pops up—*thank God*!

"My folder's really right there!" LC exclaims. "All we've got to do is open it, find the file where the memories are stored, then hook up my Cogitec port for the upload!"

"And you know how to do it all, including the hooking up and uploading?" I ask to be sure. The last thing I want us to do is damage her further.

"In theory." LC laughs nervously. "Tess loved to talk about her own brilliance when I lived with her, including explaining how things work. So I know the general steps well enough."

LC stabs a finger onto the touch screen herself.

A list of file names pops up—what at first looks like a jumble of numbers and random letters. LC leans closer, scanning it.

My eyes cross as I struggle to make sense of it when my gaze catches on something. One of the file names. Long and mostly numbers, but toward the end of it, a name.

Elaine Sasha Carter.

I freeze.

Elaine Sasha Carter.

Disbelief rocks through me. I've known that name since I was little. And here it is, identifying a file that's linked to LC. An identical first name, okay, sure. Identical middle or last names wouldn't mean a thing either. But the exact first, middle, *and* last name—and we're the same age. . . .

Memories flood through me: the world's longest waterslide, a bouncy castle, watermelon Popsicles, sleepovers with matching pj's, s'mores, American Girl dolls, and glamping tents . . .

I turn to LC. I peer into her brown-green eyes, and I finally realize why their shade was so familiar when we visited Jade in Brighthaven. Another memory floats into my mind. This one of a never-ending argument: me promising a little girl with LC's eyes that their hue is gorgeous and don't make her stick out. The little girl insisting that my brown eyes are prettier. . . .

Before I can say anything, the monitor goes dark.

"Shit!" LC shouts.

I press my fingers against the hot corner. The screen doesn't reactivate.

An alarm blares through the room.

Twenty-Six

I look at LC, panicked. "Shit! Did we trigger that with the computer?! Do you know how to disable it?!" The *wah-wah-wah* of the alarm fills the air.

LC's expression is grim. "There's nothing we can do." She gestures at the computer monitor, still dark. "I think Tess activated the lab's poison protocol."

"The what?" I ask. That *cannot* be in any way good. "And how the hell would Tess be able to activate anything when she's handcuffed?"

LC's eyes—now wide and spooked—dart to the main door. "We need to get out of here!"

But panic roots me to the floor. The building alarm is blaring. Police will be on their way. The police *cannot* come. Not while I'm in Meadows's body. If Tess *hasn't* gotten free, how will I explain why a teenage girl is handcuffed to a file cabinet in *my* supposed office? *Oh God.* If I get arrested in Tess's body, I might end up stuck in it for real!

"Megan!" LC shakes me. Hard. "Did you hear me? *We've gotta fucking go!*"

Footsteps echo beyond the door. They don't sound like they're right outside, but they don't sound very far away. I look at LC, still frozen. She grips my hand, pulls me toward the door. My mind kicks back into gear and we race from the room, the bag of Cogitec slung over LC's shoulder.

"The office," I breathe when we're a distance down the hall. "We need to get there and swap her and me."

Of course, if we get there and Tess has gotten free . . .

When we reach the office, Meadows and Jade are still inside, and Tess remains handcuffed to the cabinet. *Thank God.* But she's shifted closer to the nearby desk. She shoots a smug look at LC. Jade is standing beside her, stricken.

"She kicked some sort of button under the desk!" Jade cries. "Then the alarm went off. I'm sorry! I didn't even see what she was aiming for at first!"

LC's jaw is tight. "Tess definitely initiated the poison protocol," she says through clenched teeth. "It's why the computer shut down."

"Computer?" Jade asks.

"The one we were using in the lab," I say. "It died."

"There's an emergency button under the desk," LC explains. "It destroys all the Cogitec files and programs on any computer in the lab." As she speaks, her devastation is clear. "It's for in case the lab gets busted or the wrong person finds out about it." She swallows. "My . . . memories . . . everything she took related to my parents . . . it's now all gone. Forever."

LC's grief hits me like a dropkick to the sternum. And for a split second the name *Elaine Sasha Carter* flashes in my mind. But I push all of that aside—can't think or feel or do anything about it now.

"Did you think I wouldn't know where you two went?" Tess drawls. "I'm sure you understand, LC. I couldn't have you in there stealing any files or information. I certainly can't trust what you'd do with it."

LC balls her hands into fists. She looks like she's torn between wanting to cry and wanting to strangle Tess. But then she spins to face me. "We need to get you back into your body before the police get here!" she says.

"Immediately," Tess agrees. "And I need to be uncuffed." While she might've been desperate enough to activate the poison protocol while inside my body, she clearly doesn't want to be trapped as me any more than I want to be trapped as her.

LC starts to rummage in the bag for the Cogitec equipment we'll need. As she does, a new fear washes over me.

I desperately want to get the switch over with, of course. To finally, finally, *finally* get my body back. And we do need to make it happen before the police arrive. But, despite the urgency, what happens after we leave the building in our own bodies? I don't believe for one second that Tess will just forget about us and trust we'll keep our mouths shut. She already knows Jade's address, and she knows that I live somewhere in Graysonville. Not only that her gun is still in the room. After we swap back, what if she's desperate enough to somehow *kill* me, Jade, and LC, so that we don't talk?

So, what the hell do I do to make sure we're *safe?* And how am I supposed to figure it out with the cops on the way and the alarm blasting?

I remind myself how strong I've been already throughout this entire nightmare. I remind myself how fierce I can be.

Then I realize something: Maybe tripping the alarm didn't make things *messier*! Maybe it makes everything *simpler*.

"Give me your phone!" I bark at LC. She hands me the phone (my phone, really, since it's "Megan's"), and I log into Instagram. I pull up the screen to post a Reel and hand the phone back to LC. "Take a video when I say so," I tell her. "Save it to my drafts folder. We need to get this done before the police arrive."

I look at Tess in my body, arm in a cast, cuffed helplessly to the cabinet—and I can't believe what I'm gonna do.

"Record now," I say to LC, swallowing the bitter taste in my mouth.

I give myself no time to reconsider. I turn to Tess. "Megan," I say, "I kidnapped you and brought you to this office because nobody will be able to find you here until it's too late."

And before she can respond, I fly at her.

"I'll kill you, Megan Allen!" I scream. "I fucking swear!"

With the video recording, I start punching and kicking my own body. Tess tries to shield herself with her one free arm, screaming at me to stop. When my cheek splits open and blood rushes down my face, I want to stop. But I steel myself to keep going—because that's not the worst of what I need to do. I wrap "Tess's" hands around "Megan Allen's" neck and squeeze. She claws at the back of my hands, gasping for air.

"What the fuck?!" Jade sobs. "What the fuck?! Why the fuck are you doing that?!"

"I get why, and it's enough!" LC hollers. "Stop, Megan! God, please stop! I just cut the video!"

Twenty-Seven

I back away from Tess, chest heaving.

Sprawled on the floor, she holds her throat—*my* throat—breathing raggedly. She stares at me in disbelief as she hauls herself up to sit and sags against the side of the cabinet. My right eye is bruised; there's a gash under it and one across my chin. For a second, all I can do is stare right back. Outside of that small scuffle with LC, I've never thrown a punch or been on the receiving end of one before. Now I've accomplished both at the same freaking time—my own body having absorbed the blows that I, myself, landed. *Wild.* It looks as if I've gone a round in a boxing ring.

"We're swapping now," I tell Tess, swallowing hard, beyond ready to end this entire crazy-ass nightmare.

LC is immediately at my side, holding a Cogitec gun. *I've got it,* I want to say, because I still want to remain in control. But LC has the experience with the tech, and this is too big to risk jacking something up. So I nod yes when she asks if I'm ready.

First, she presses the Cogitec gun to Tess's neck. I hear a slight click, and Tess slumps forward a little farther—still awake but briefly drained. Next, it's my turn.

I feel the press of the gun against the barbell. Then, like before, there's the moment of extreme weakness—the moment when LC downloads a copy of my consciousness. After that, LC returns to my real body and presses the gun against its neck a second time.

"Okay, here goes," she says to me.

My world goes blank. When it comes back into focus, I'm sitting on the floor, handcuffed to the cabinet. My face throbs like hell, and my neck burns like it's on fire, but I don't care because the pain means I'm inside my own body. *My* body! I'm me! *I'm me again!* I grin like a fool, despite how much it hurts to do it. I'd literally hug myself if I could. I reach up and touch my mouth; my lips have the shape and fullness I've always known. And my racing heartbeat, the pulse thumping in my ears, the tingles shooting along my skin from happiness—all of it is precisely how those sensations should sound and feel to *Megan*! I wiggle the fingers on my good hand and imagine I'm playing the piano and grin harder because they plink against invisible keys with an easy and masterful dexterity. I. Am. Megan. *Finally.*

I steal one more second to be joyful, to be *grateful*, and then I place it aside. There's something crucial left for me to do. And if I know LC, it's not going to be easy.

I gaze at Tess, who's now lying crumpled on the floor beside LC's feet. Well . . . *Tess's body*, that is. LC hasn't reinserted Tess's consciousness, so her body is simply an empty shell. Still as death. LC looks down at her with zero pity.

Please let me be convincing.

"I need you to put her microchip inside her, LC," I say. "I need you to upload her consciousness."

LC grips the gun. "Hell no. Why would we do that?"

"Because anything else means you've killed her," I say. "You said how hard it was for you to know you'd hurt me and Jade. Well, *murdering* Tess goes far beyond anything you've already done."

"I promise you, I won't lose sleep over Tess," LC snaps. "And even if I would, that can't matter; she's too dangerous to leave alive!"

"That's what the video's for," I say. "So we can get her put away! I didn't beat up my own body for fun!"

LC shakes her head. "I filmed you in case we needed it, but I'm dealing with Tess, right here and right now—in my own way. You'll thank me later when you and Jade are really, truly safe and back living your old lives, like I promised, *without* having to always look over your shoulder for Tess. Trust me, you don't wanna live that way."

"And how do *you* wanna live after we get out of here?" I reply. I have to reach her—she's *Sasha*. I can't let her wreck her life more.

"That doesn't matter, either," LC spits bitterly. "I can live with leaving Tess's chip out. Fuck her! I *can't* live with not making up for what I did to you and Jade *all the way*." Her expression softens a bit as she looks at me. "Let me do this for y'all, Megan. *Please.* You and Jade can run now. I'll stay behind. Let the cops arrest me for whatever they assume I did to Tess. That keeps you, Jade, and me forever safe from her, *and* I get even with Tess. That's *all* that counts."

"You'll go to prison—"

"Yeah, but if we go with your plan—which I assume is to reinsert her chip and let the police arrest her for assaulting you—"

"And kidnapping," I add. "Across state lines."

"Still, it's not foolproof," LC says. "Especially when you're Black and she's a privileged, rich-ass white woman—one who won't stop at *anything*. How long do you really think she'd go away for, if she goes at all?"

"Maybe a long time," I argue desperately. "She could!" But even though I say it, I know LC's got a damn convincing point.

"We both know better," LC says. "Plus, I deserve whatever I get as much as Tess does." Her demeanor has become alarmingly stoic. "Let this be how *I* pay. What life would I have after today, anyway? I'm an orphan with no home, no family, nothing. I refuse to go back to foster care, so I'd just be back on the streets. Prison means somewhere to sleep, regular meals, and Tess gets neutralized forever." She sounds so broken, so defeated, so exhausted when she says it.

And I know more than ever that I cannot leave her behind. *It's just not right.* I'm pretty sure I'd feel this way even if she wasn't Sasha.

I wish I could tell LC what I suspect about her real identity, but the building alarm is still blaring and time is running out, and God knows that's going to be a huge revelation—too much to put out there right now.

"You're wrong," I say. "You don't deserve prison. You were taken advantage of, abused, actually, and you deserve a second chance. I know why you want Tess to pay. And *she* should pay.

You committing murder isn't the way, though. *Please* care about yourself more. You *can* have a future. A good one. I'll help you get there. But we can't figure it out if you do this to Tess."

LC stares at me with a deeply conflicted expression.

"It will damage *you* more than her," I continue. "Don't give her that power. *Please.* Let's just restore her consciousness and show the video to the police. You're right: they might not give a shit about some white lady beating me. But they will absolutely care about Tess impersonating a federal agent. Her badge proves she did it. And that, by itself, should put Tess in jail for a good, long time."

LC still doesn't say anything, but I see the slightest shift in her eyes.

"If you're really sorry for what you did to me and Jade," I say, "do what I want. That's how I'm asking you to make it good. I was your victim, so I get a say in how I want you to pay, right?"

LC bites her lip, considering. "What about you?" she asks Jade. "Megan can't speak for you, and I'm sure you want—"

"You can't speak for me, either, LC," Jade says. "Megan is right. I'm not supporting murder."

As we stand looking at each other, all of a sudden there's a reverberating silence. The alarm stopped blaring.

"That might mean the police are here!" I say. "LC, *please*. Do it now."

"Okay," she says softly. "If that's what you both want. Okay."

She grabs Tess by the arm, touches the gun to Tess's barbell, and keeps it pressed against the spot. Tess's eyes flutter then open. After looking wildly around the room, clearly disoriented, she snaps her attention to LC. Her gaze narrows viciously as she pushes to sit up.

LC slams a hand into her chest when she tries to stand and warns, "Don't move another inch. Let yourself be arrested, or, I swear to God, I'll tell them everything about Cogitec."

Tess glowers but doesn't try anything.

"Go outside and bring the police here," I tell Jade. "And toss this in a dumpster." I kick the bag with the remaining Cogitec. It's not where I'd have wanted to dispose of it—not secure enough. But with the police coming, we don't really have a choice. I'm not even tempted to try to get them—or even the real FBI—to believe what it's used for. The sooner I have nothing to do with Cogitec, the better. I have zero confidence that LC, Jade, and I would be safe being witnesses in some sort of investigation into Tess and any other people involved in Cogitec's development.

Jade rushes out. Tess looks between me and LC.

"You really think getting me arrested is going to protect you?" she says. "I thought you were smarter than that. Guess I was wrong."

We don't take her bait, but I hate knowing that she might be right.

When Jade returns with the cops, I put on what I hope is one of the last performances I'll have to do. LC tells them Tess is a sort of foster parent to her, that she's abusive. She says that I—Megan—helped her run away from Tess, which is what caused Tess to do this to me. I tell them that Tess lied and told me she was an FBI agent to get me to trust her; we've set out the fake badge on the desk to prove it. I tell them that she lured me into her car by asking me to help her locate LC so she could help protect her. Finally, I add that I met LC on the internet and had never seen Tess in person before—that Tess only told me who she really was when we got to her office and in a fit of rage tried to kill me for taking LC away from her. The story is a bit convoluted, but between my injuries and the video, the police seem to believe us.

Tess is led from the room. Before she crosses the threshold, she says over her shoulder, "I hope you know what you're doing; there are much more dangerous things than me in this world for a girl who has to fend for herself, LC."

To the cops, I'm sure it sounds only like crap gaslighting from a manipulative guardian. But I read the true threat loud and clear: We may have neutralized Tess for the moment, but the Cogitec investors she's mentioned before—the powerful, dangerous ones—are still out there. And even if we're safe from Tess, we won't be safe from them.

Twenty-Eight

After I've been checked out and bandaged up at the hospital, and we're blessedly waiting for my real parents—the *Allens*, not the *McCalls*—to arrive, I finally have the time and presence of mind to tell LC the impossible connection I realized in the lab when we opened her file. It's still nearly too unbelievable to wrap my mind around. *God*, I wish I had realized why those hazel eyes looked so damn familiar when I visited Jade in the group home. If I had, LC would've had somebody *really* in her corner from that moment on.

"I'm so, so sorry we couldn't upload your memories," I begin, sitting up straighter in the emergency room bed. Dull pain lingers from when I kicked myself in the chest. I instinctively cradle it.

LC leans forward in her nearby chair, reaching for the call button on the remote next to my knee. "Do you need me to get the nurse? They should've given you better pain meds. What the fuck is ibuprofen gonna do?" Anger wrinkles her forehead—and it's an expression I use to see all the time from my sassy friend Sasha when something upset her. Back then, I'd always do something goofy in response, because I knew her laughter would wipe away whatever she was upset about. I hated seeing Elaine Sasha Carter hurt or mad or sad about anything.

A lump forms in my throat like I've swallowed a rock. "The Motrin tablets were good," I say. I shimmy in my bed gingerly to prove my point and make her stop worrying. Right now isn't about me. It's about her, and I don't want her to be distracted.

"What is it, then? You're all . . . worked up. I can tell." LC scans me with growing concern.

"You deserve to have your memories back. They're your entire past. Your history. Who you were before Tess," I start again.

"The files are still on a cloud drive," she cuts in softly. "So, maybe someday, if we can figure out how to access them, without the lab computer . . ."

I nod. "The thing is . . . I can fill in some of the missing details for you without it."

She stares at me, confused. The way she lowers her eyebrows to express puzzlement gives me another little jolt of recognition. My old best friend did that all the time, too.

"Do you know your full name?" I ask. "Or birthday? How much info did Tess take from you?"

"Um . . . it's Lainey Carter, right? And . . . I think I was born in April. That's all I know." She shrugs like it's no big deal, like Tess didn't carve out enormous, precious pieces of her and leave gaping holes behind. Her face has crumpled in a way that says different.

My hands curl into fists. But again, this isn't about me. I shake off the fury and take out my phone, which LC returned

251

to me. I log into the family iCloud photo account and search by year. I go back to my childhood days, eagerly scanning the images, heart pumping with anticipation. . . .

"Look!" I say, and forget to keep my voice down.

LC studies the picture on the screen—two little girls, one dressed as Alice in Wonderland and one dressed as the Dormouse. The pair—tight as thieves, thick as sisters—smile so wide, their eyes twinkle. They're different from how they look now but still recognizable.

"I don't understand," LC murmurs, dumbstruck. "Is that . . . ?"

"Yeah," I breathe. "That's us!" I smile as wide as in the picture, my eyes burning. "Your full name is Elaine Sasha Carter. That picture was taken on my birthday, April eleventh, when I turned six. You turned six the day before."

Her eyes jump to me, wide and full of hope. Searching. "And I was . . . at your party?"

"Of course. We'd never have missed each other's parties."

The stages of shock that keep appearing on her face make me laugh; I'm deliriously happy and so thankful that I can give her back some pieces of herself.

"I know, it's wild that we knew each other before," I say. "Beyond wild. But our parents were best friends. And me and you were inseparable from when we were babies until we were six. Our stupid parents stopped speaking after some huge falling-out, and then you and your parents moved out of Graysonville. You moving was the worst day of my life. We were the closest of friends. We'd tell folks we were sisters. We loved each other."

Her gobsmacked expression doesn't change. She's staring at me like this is all taking time to sink in. Which of course it is.

"Seriously, we loved each other so much. We'd play in our backyards and go roller-skating and to the water park. . . . We haven't seen each other since the falling-out, of course," I say gently. I didn't even know her parents had died. I don't think Mom and Dad know either. That's something they would've told me. "It was a long time ago, and the memories are a little fuzzy," I admit. "But I've wondered a lot about where you moved and thought about finding you on social media. I even tried searching a few times for Sasha Carter—that's the name you went by. I called you Sash. You called me Meggie."

LC shakes her head, looks at her feet. "Maybe when I came to Graysonville . . . Maybe that's why I picked Graysonville and you, Megan, in the first place? Maybe it wasn't random at all?" She winces after she says it, her entire posture curving in on itself under the weight of obvious guilt.

I cup her face and force her eyes back to me, where she can see in my eyes how much I mean it when I say: "It could have been. Your memories were stolen, but there was something deep inside leading you home. I don't give a crap about anything else. It's behind us. I only care that I have you back."

She bites her lip as it begins to tremble. "I didn't fake our friendship and the bond we formed, Megan. That was one-hundred-percent real for me. Whenever we hung out, I felt so at home with you, and I guess our past explains why." She's quiet for a moment, considering something. "I think it also explains the reason I changed my plan and wanted to swap back with you and

Jade. . . . It was really difficult, pretending to be you, lying all the time, taking your family from you. I thought I'd feel so at peace in your home, with parents who loved me. But I just felt ashamed and shitty as hell." She pauses. "Of course I know what I did was wrong regardless! But it was different with you than with Jade. I felt so much worse and couldn't bury my guilt. I can't say I'm sorry enough."

I swallow the lump in my throat.

"Also," LC adds, "I want you to know I *never* would've ruined your life or your family's life for good, like I threatened. I was just desperate and bluffing."

I don't need the gutted expression on LC's face to know that she's telling the truth. I swear I *feel* her honesty reverberate in my soul—like we're actually linked in some preternatural way. I muse how I called us "best friend soulmates" back when I met her as LC—when I knew nothing of her being Sasha.

I suppose that a supernatural bond between people is *highly* implausible, but then again . . . a lot of seemingly *highly* implausible things have occurred and turned out to be possible. So, maybe my deepest inner self, my *soul*, did recognize who LC really was to me; maybe that *was* the true reason for the automatic and super-strong connection I formed with her.

That's wild—and extraordinary—to think about. But I set aside the wonder for the moment, because I have one more thing that I need to share with LC. I bring her attention back to the photo of us.

"Look," I say.

MEGAN ZOOMS IN on the photo of the two of them in their *Alice in Wonderland* costumes, slides it to focus on a face behind the little girls. A woman. Tears sting LC's eyes because she knows. She knows. It's the face that she always draws. The one that the pencil always wants to form, even though LC has never known why. Until right this moment.

Megan says gently what LC has already concluded: "That's your mom. You've been drawing her face. I hadn't looked at these pictures in a long time, so I didn't make the connection." Megan reaches for her hand and squeezes it. "I know we can't get your parents back, and maybe not your memories, either. But at least now you'll have me. My family too."

LC is speechless. She stares at the photo a few precious seconds longer, then looks at Megan, feeling the tears splash onto her cheeks.

After Tess, she didn't know if she could ever truly have a real life, a normal life, again. But she's so glad Megan is convincing her to try. Because these photos make her want one. Megan's given her so many gifts. LC's regained her self. Her past. Her parents, in some way. A friend and sister who stood beside LC and fought for her when LC was incapable of fighting for herself—even when she was acting foul toward Megan. LC can never repay Megan enough. But she'll start by striving to become a better person who makes better choices.

Somebody worthy of Megan's decision to help LC when she didn't have to.

Twenty-Nine

"Megan?"

The choked voice is my dad's. I'm so grateful to hear his warm, deep timbre that tears sting my eyes. He, my mother, and Sophie hurry toward the hospital bed.

"It's me!" I sputter. "*It's me.* I'm so glad you're here!" I've never, ever been more overjoyed to see them. "I'm totally okay," I assure my mom when her arms lock around me in a mama-bear-fierce grip. I inhale her scent, let her favorite vanilla and coconut soap enfold me. I already told her and Dad over the phone that I was fine when the hospital called them. But I know Mom; she was definitely drowning in panic until she saw the truth with her own eyes.

When she finally lets me go, she gazes at me intently, and I know she's searching to make sure I'm not downplaying how bad I feel.

"Okay," she says after checking me over head to toe twice.

"She really seems all right." Relief pours from her as she tells Dad this.

He hugs me next. I lean into the feel of his trimmed beard scratching my cheek. When it's Sophie's turn, I bury my face in the little troll's hair, drag my good hand through her curls. "I love you so much," I tell her.

Sophie pulls away. "Are you sure you're okay?" she asks, looking skeptical. I laugh.

As I do, I notice LC, who's staring at her feet, fidgeting with the knee of her jeans. I grab her hand and look back at my family.

"I have someone to introduce to you," I tell them. "Well, reintroduce." I pause to give LC a moment to prepare for what's about to happen. When she gives me a tiny but grateful smile that's permission to go on, I say, "Mom, Dad, Soph . . . this is Sasha."

Epilogue

Three weeks later, I sit on my couch beside Sasha and Sophie playing *Ghosts of Saturn*, spending quality time with my little sister without complaint. Soph even insisted that I use her shiny new pink Xbox controller. As Sophie's own alien-battling avatar carries me—she's doing all the work because my *punch-shoot-stab-kick* coordination sucks—I smile down at the controller that drained my savings. Holding it should make me ill. It is, after all, intrinsically linked to the nape piercing and the body swap. Had I not bribed Soph to keep quiet when she barged in on me and LC, she would've blabbed to Mom and Dad that night and they would've kicked LC out and grounded me for literal life.

But I can't dredge up regret. Miraculously, some good came from it all: I got my oldest, bestest friend back. Plus, I discovered some pretty impressive things about myself—stuff that I was far from recognizing before all of this. Not to mention, I gained a badass scar on my chin. (Okay, it's almost invisible already, but whatever. It was there. And it's *fierce*—like me.)

"Megan! Do something! HIT SOMETHING! SHOOT SOMETHING!" Sophie rails, snapping me out of my thoughts. "Ugh! You're gonna make us get overrun by space zombies! I need a better partner," she grumbles, her face twisted in the intense way it gets when she's laser-focused on a game.

"Sorry?" I offer, while Sasha chuckles. Did I mention I suck at video games? And I can't use the excuse of trying to play one-handed; my cast came off two days ago, *thank goodness*.

Sophie sighs, pauses the game, and sticks her hand out. "This was a fun idea to play together, and thanks, Meggie, for trying, but nah. You ain't gonna mess up my stats. Nobody will team up with me in co-op mode with garbage numbers." She keeps her hand out, waiting for me to give up her precious controller.

I clutch my chest like I'm wounded. "Ouch, little sis! Really?"

She pops her lips pointedly and wholly unapologetically.

I grin. "I missed you. A lot." I lunge for her and pull her into a hug.

She pretends like she's choking. "Too tight, dork." She giggles.

I squeeze her tighter. "How about this?"

She shoves me off, then smacks me in the face with a couch pillow. "What's gotten into you since you got home from the hospital?" She pokes the center of my forehead. "Did an alien species hijack your brain? Are you *sure* you're my real sister?"

Sophie is only playing around, being her normal *extra* self. But her joke skates uncomfortably close to the truth. Also, my little sister is brilliant, and she's already been adamant that something is fishy about the story LC and I told my parents and the ·ops. She hasn't expressed anything to Mom and Dad, *thank God*, but she keeps finding times to slip into my room and interrogate me. She's been interrogating Sasha (who's living with us now), too, unable to decide if she's stoked to have a new sibling or disgruntled she has to share the upstairs bathroom with another person.

"I can play. I'm pretty good at video games. I mean . . . if you want me to?" Sasha says to Sophie now. She's been making every attempt possible to get Sophie to warm up to her. Sometimes her gestures work. Sometimes Sophie pretends Sasha isn't around.

She rolls her eyes but plops the controller in Sasha's hand. "You better actually be good," she warns Sasha.

Sasha winks. "I'll prove myself to you, Baby Boss Bitch. Just wait and see!"

I'll prove myself to you: it's the same promise she's offered up to me a dozen times since we've come home. She knows I've forgiven her—I've told her that every time she's apologized. But she still feels guilty and is being stubborn about needing to do more to make up for what she did to me and Jade.

A cool thing that's come out of this whole experience: she's been wondering about majoring in psychology if she goes to college so she can become a therapist for girls like she used to be. *Not a predatory fake like Tess*, she says, *but a* real *therapist who gives the kind of help I could've used.*

While Sasha and Sophie are kicking butt, I pull up the text thread that's been renewed after a year of silence between Ava and me. Something else good that came of the body-swapping nightmare: Ava and I have been texting each other a decent bit—mostly nerdy sci-fi and anime memes. We haven't hung out yet, but I'd like to change that.

Do you want to come over? I write. Sophie and Sasha are gaming, but we can watch Sailor Moon Eternal or Riverdale or Star Wars.

No matter what happens between us, I've definitely learned that ride-or-die friends are vital to have. Ava really showed up for me when I was in trouble—like she always did when we were friends. I should have valued her more.

Ellipses pop up under my latest text; I draw in a breath, hopeful.

I'll be over in ten. Can we make it Sailor Moon Crystal?

I bounce a little in happiness. Can't wait, I type back. And yes! Whatever you want! I'm in the mood for a Crystal rewatch too!

"Ava's on her way to watch *Sailor Moon* with me," I tell Soph and Sasha. "You want to join?"

Engrossed in her game, Sophie only shrugs, too focused to do anything else.

"You can come up later too," I tell Sasha, not wanting to leave her out if she and Soph finish their gaming session before Ava goes home.

"I'm good," Sasha says. "It might take a while to prove myself worthy of this controller I've been blessed with." She winks at Sophie.

Sophie snorts but doesn't argue about Sasha lingering for an extended time. In fact, she tells her, "I'm holding you hostage for at least five rounds if you're really out to prove something, sis."

I grin at the pair of them finally bonding, then head out.

I take the stairs to my room two at a time. In my good mood, I decide to take advantage of the moment alone.

"Hey!" I say to Ryan when he answers the FaceTime call. I'm breathless in a way that's not from running upstairs. I can't even fake it, nor do I want to. My irregular breathing has everything to do with this boy's unfairly gorgeous face, his full, kissable lips, and his blinding smile.

"Hey yourself," he tells me, grinning wider. I'm not the only one who sounds breathless.

Good.

"How was practice?" I ask.

"Brutal. Coach made us run three miles, then kicked our butts some more with suicides because two of the guys are failing and it pissed him off. But I offered to tutor them, so their grades should be up before spring ball starts."

"You're amazing. You know that? All around."

He quirks an eyebrow. "*I'm* amazing. I think you meant to say that *you*, as in Megan Allen, are amazing. Jade returned to school today finally, by the way. She says hi. She's doing good. Better than good, really. She's patching things over with her old Woodard crew and has this new crush who isn't a douche. I keep saying this, but thank you. *Thank you.*"

"I didn't do anything I did for a thanks," I say awkwardly. "But, umm . . . you're welcome."

"I've been meaning to ask you something." The sheepish way Ryan says it makes me curious.

"What?"

"I . . . err . . . wanted to see if maybe you want to hang out with me sometime? We haven't seen each other since, you know, and I . . . errr . . . I miss you. I can drive down to Graysonville? We can do whatever you want."

I don't think it's possible for me to cheese harder. "Are you asking me on a date?" I tease. Then I want to facepalm my head because of course he is. *Of-freaking-course he is!*

I do a happy shimmy, not caring that it's dorky *and* that he sees it. The happy, shimmying, rhythmless geek girl is me. It's what he's gonna get if he's going on a date with Megan Allen.

"Do you want to check out the BlerdGeeks Con that'll be in downtown Atlanta this weekend?" I ask.

"Sounds cool. I'm there!" Ryan answers. "And, um, I wanted to ask something else too."

"Okay . . ." The wariness in his voice makes me freeze.

"Has anything, you know, weird happened since you've been home?" From his tone, I know he's referring to Tess's threat. This is his way of asking if anybody shady has come around or if anything else alarming has gone down.

"No," I say, nervous. "Has Jade—"

"No," he says quickly. "No, don't worry. I was just checking."

My racing heart slows. But the spike of fear reminds me that no matter how fantastic things are going, the way I move through life will never be the same again. Even though LC and I removed our piercings as soon as we got to my house, I don't think I'll ever feel free from my connection to Cogitec. Whenever I'm out in public, I can't shake the feeling that I'm being tracked. Every time I see a black Volvo, I go cold. And at night, whenever the house is ⸱rk and I hear little bumps or knocks, I nearly jump out of my skin and have to turn on every light around me. Will those things ever change? I want them to so I can feel one-hundred-percent normal again, but I don't see how they can.

Sasha has made it clear to me that Tess really does have wealthy, powerful investors—people even *Tess* feared, apparently. Like I thought, they're the danger Tess warned us about when the police took her away. And then there's Tess herself. She hasn't had her trial yet, but even if she does go to prison, she still could resurface at any time, in any body. I wouldn't put anything past her.

I quash the thoughts. There's no immediate danger. I should let myself enjoy being a regular teen on the phone with a guy she likes, planning her first real date.

Live in the moment, behave normally, be happy. That's what Sasha, Jade, and I decided we'd do to move forward and not let fear trash our futures.

And if danger comes, we've got a game plan for that too. . . .

Much like I underestimated myself, Tess underestimated the force that the three of us girls could be when we banded together. And our strength doesn't lie in how physically strong we may or may not be, either. It's soul-deep; no one can take it from us.

We are fierce. We are epic. We are bold.

And all of us are survivors.

Acknowledgments

Since I first started writing with the dream of publishing books that would make their way into the world and be read by others, publishing a YA story was at the top of my *wildest dreams* list. I've always had an immense love for YA books, and I am thankful to all the individuals who helped me on this journey.

First and foremost, I must thank my rockstar agent, Caitie Flum, who 1000% supports each and every one of my dreams related to writing. Thank you so much for always being my champion and cheerleader! To Marianna, my amazing editor at Dovetail Fiction who helped conceive this story and worked with me to bring it to life in such a powerful way, an immense thank-you! I am always in awe of your editorial insight. A huge thank-you to Lynn at Dovetail Fiction as well for supporting my vision for Megan's and LC's story. To Tiara Kittrell, I am forever grateful that you saw something special in this story and bought it. To Donna Bray and the entire Balzer + Bray team, thank you for believing in this dream project of mine also. I am so grateful for everyone's support and enthusiasm for this novel!

As always, this is one more story that would not have come together without my extraordinary friends who are also my writing peeps: Traci-Anne, Shari, Kwame, Liz, Jamar, Alaysia, Andre, Davaun, and Brent—I am always grateful to you for taking the time to read pages, provide feedback, or just be an ear to bounce ideas off. To Liz especially, you were amazing and so vital on this journey as I wrote my first thriller ever. There were a lot of tears, a lot of growing pains, and a lot of anxiety about nailing this story, and you helped me remain positive and confident in a huge way!

Lastly, to any readers who may be coming to this story after reading my previous books, the biggest of THANK-YOUs for picking up *Out of Body* and continuing to come along with me on this writing journey!